A1290 80384

WITHDRAWN

THE IMAGINATION'S
PROVOCATION: VOLUME I

To the Students of ICC,

Best Wishes!

Yours,

Scott William Foley

The following selections, previously published:

"The Story of Corporal Foley" Copyright © 2003 S. William Foley

"The Marble Man" Copyright © 2003 S. William Foley

"The Bridewell House" Copyright © 2003 S. William Foley

"Trees" Copyright © 2003 S. William Foley

"The Runner" Copyright © 2003 S. William Foley

"Suffocation" Copyright © 2004 S. William Foley

"Proposing to Krissy" Copyright © 2004 S. William Foley

"Freedom's Resurrection: from the Chronicles of Purgatory Station" Copyright © 2004 S. William Foley

"The Jhudo Rite" Copyright © 2004 S. William Foley

"Graffiti" Copyright © 2004 S. William Foley

"Dispute at the Paragon Tree" Copyright © 2004 S. William Foley

"Voices" Copyright © 2004 S. William Foley

"Severed Wires" Copyright © 2004 S. William Foley

"Hello, My Name Is Zoe" Copyright © 2004 S. William Foley

www.swilliamfoley.com

THE IMAGINATION'S PROVOCATION: VOLUME I

A Collection of Short Stories

S. William Foley

I.C.C. LIBRARY

iUniverse, Inc.

New York Lincoln Shanghai

PS
48
S5
65
2005
v. 1

THE IMAGINATION'S PROVOCATION: VOLUME I
A Collection of Short Stories

Copyright © 2005 by Scott William Foley

All rights reserved. No part of this book may be used or reproduced by any means, graphic, electronic, or mechanical, including photocopying, recording, taping or by any information storage retrieval system without the written permission of the publisher except in the case of brief quotations embodied in critical articles and reviews.

iUniverse books may be ordered through booksellers or by contacting:

iUniverse
2021 Pine Lake Road, Suite 100
Lincoln, NE 68512
www.iuniverse.com
1-800-Authors (1-800-288-4677)

This book is a work of fiction.
Names, characters, places, and incidents either are products of the author's imagination or are being used fictitiously.
Any resemblance to actual events or locales or persons, living or dead, is entirely coincidental or used with permission.

ISBN: 0-595-34472-0

Printed in the United States of America

4/09 B&T 12.95

Contents

Special Thanks

My Lord and Savior, Jesus Christ

My Wife, Kristen Foley

My Mom, Connie Foley

My Dad, Ross Foley

My First Publisher, Pete Moore

My Family

My Friends

My Readers

A Note From the Author

So, this is it!

I hate to sound overly giddy, but what you hold in your hands right now is a dream of mine that has existed for a very long time that has finally come to fruition.

Let me start at the beginning. My name is Scott. As far as my writing goes, I go by S. William for several reasons. One, there is an actor called Scott Foley and I didn't want anyone getting me confused with him. Secondly, it sounds more literary to me. I hope that's not pompous, but I can't help it, one of my favorite writers is F. Scott Fitzgerald. To me, it just sounds better. But, for the record, my name is Scott William Foley.

At any rate, I'm a high school English teacher who has always dreamed of being a fiction writer. I've loved virtually any and all forms of fiction for as long as I can remember, and I'm overjoyed to finally be contributing my voice to the ranks.

When I was a senior at Illinois State University, I was getting closer and closer to graduating. I suppose I freaked out a little at the prospect of joining the "professional" crowd. I went to speak with a career counselor and she asked me what I'd like to do if I didn't have to immediately join the working world. I answered that I'd always wanted to write a novel. She asked me if I had any ideas in mind, and I told her that, in fact, I did. So, I went through what was essentially a story pitch to a woman who had no link to the publishing world whatsoever! At any rate, after hearing the idea for the story, she said that although she technically wasn't encouraged to tell students to lay off work for a while, she urged me to set a timeline for myself and then write my story. I couldn't believe it!

Well, thankfully, my parents are two of the most compassionate people I know. After I graduated in December of 1999, they urged me to follow my dream as well and they let me move back home to write at night and substitute teach during the day. I did just that, and within six months, I had written my first novel, *Souls Triumphant*. Little did I realize that writing a novel and publishing a novel were actually two TOTALLY different things!

So, I soon found myself in the working world as a professional teacher. A few years had passed, my novel simply gathered dust, and my writing had begun and ended with that one novel. I had aborted my dream.

But then I met my wife in 2002.

She read my novel and really wanted me to begin writing again. The nice thing about being a teacher, besides trying to make the world a better place than when you found it, is having three months of the year to do with as you will.

At her behest, I began writing short stories to submit to magazines. Once again, I met with rejection letter after rejection letter. However, the wonderful thing was that I learned I did have more than one story in me; in fact, I could write virtually anywhere, anytime. This was very welcome news.

And then the ball really got rolling. While hanging out with some friends, I met a guy named Pete Moore who happened to own and operate a website called bloomingtonnormal.com. He needed writers, as I came to find out, so I did yet another impromptu story pitch. He liked what I had to say and invited me to submit some of my works to him.

From that moment on, I began being published at bloomingtonnormal.com every month under the column "The Imagination's Provocation." It was awesome! It was also quite hard! Dreaming up a story idea, plotting it, writing it, proofing and revising it, and then publishing it on a monthly basis was and still is very demanding. I loved it though, and delivered for over a year without missing a deadline. I am currently on a break as I am putting this little diddy together, but will soon begin again on the monthly writings. I am forever indebted to Pete for publishing me and getting me started on a path that seems to be wide open.

And so, after over a year of writing short stories and having them published over the 'net, I finally decided that perhaps it was time to put my stories into book format. And thus, you have this book before you.

You'll find in this collection fantasy stories, horror stories, historical fiction, science fiction, humorous stories, and inspirational stories. I love so many different types of fiction; I can't seem to limit myself to just one! Some of them you'll love, some of them you'll hate, but I hope that there is at least one that provokes your imagination.

If this work does well, in terms of sales, you will be seeing my first novel, *Souls Triumphant*, in book format as well by July of 2005. Until then, you can read the first half of it at my website, swilliamfoley.com.

Well, I think that I have gone on and on about myself for quite long enough. Thank you for humoring me! So, enough about me—on to the stories! I truly hope that you enjoy them, and I sincerely thank you from the bottom of my heart for giving my writings a chance.

It is only with all of your support that I can continue on with my dream. Thank you.

Scott William Foley
January 15, 2005

The Story of Corporal Foley

Even though the facility was in excellent condition and quite beautiful to the eye, Jack could not help but associate it with death. Perhaps it was because of this unshakeable, though ridiculous, impression that the auburn-haired man remained in his car for several minutes. He was, indeed, desperately hoping that his parents would readily appear.

"I'm twenty-four years old," Jack finally muttered to himself with disdain, "I don't need Mom and Dad with me…"

The door to the red mustang burst open and dismissed its operator. Jack began his trek to the large, well-maintained building.

Relieved that the journey into the building was apparently successful thus far, he decided to tempt fate even further and approached an obese woman at the front desk.

"I'm here to see Meredith Finch," Jack spewed out, trying to sound relaxed while knowing that his anxiety was perfectly conspicuous.

Noticing her poorly sustained dental work, the young man listened as the rather unattractive woman smiled sincerely and said, "Three-oh-one, hon."

Jack issued forth something to the woman that was either an expression of gratitude or a sigh of nervousness and began the arduous junket to the third floor.

It was while executing this tour that Jack beheld that which caused him to experience such dismay. It's not that he wasn't experienced with social encounters. He dealt with well over two hundred people every day on a fairly personal level. It's just that the marked difference between his workweek and this Saturday's visit was the specimen of people that he was now encountering. He had grown accustomed to associating with human beings whose stories were just beginning, those who literally had yet their whole lives to live.

It was this habitual familiarity with youth that caused Jack such a lack of aptitude with his present situation. In fact, the young teacher was not very good at all in conversing with the opposite end of the spectrum of his acquaintance. The tall, young man was, as said, in the habit of dealing with those whose stories were just beginning; here all Jack saw were those whose stories were very nearly over.

He was ashamed as he walked hurriedly past the ancient people sitting in wheelchairs and lying on beds in the hallway. He was mortified that they would reach out to touch a young man like himself, and he would pull away from them. He was sickened at his own timidity as they would plead for help, and he would charge past them as though they did not even exist. Jack had always considered himself to be a role model to his students; he prayed intensely that they would never learn of his behavior in this place.

Beholden to a higher power, Jack finally reached room 301 after dashing up two flights of stairs in lieu of waiting for an elevator in the hallway with the antiquated ones.

After knocking on her door as unobtrusively as possible, Jack heard a capable, soft voice call to enter. As he passed through the doorway, the fainthearted Jack disappeared and transformed once more into his traditional persona upon seeing the charming woman sitting upright on her bed with a case placed over her lap.

"Hello, Meredith," Jack heard his customary voice say with relief as he noted the familiar dignitary. The bespectacled young man began to approach the silver-haired, petite woman for an embrace; however, before a single step could be taken, he realized upon reading her eyes that this Saturday visit was not one to begin with a hug. Instead, Jack simply placed the card he had picked up that morning on the nightstand next to Meredith's bed. Then he stood still and waited patiently.

After taking in a breath of air hurriedly, as though surprised, Meredith sung, "What's this now?" The thin, neatly dressed woman swooped up the card and tore it open, careful not to disrupt the small, thin case on her lap. "It *is* my birthday…" Meredith said with a smile as she nodded her head profusely and read the innards of the card along with Jack's signature. "Thank you, Jack," she crooned.

"You're quite welcome," Jack replied, regaled by the old woman's still remaining cleverness. Jack moved across the small room and sat in the only recliner merely a few feet from the beaming Meredith. For several moments, the two simply relaxed where they were without saying a word to one another.

Jack absent-mindedly took out the old pocket watch that had been given to him as a gift as he sat with the elderly woman in serenity. He was too young when he had received the watch to realize how monumental of a present had been bestowed upon him. Now fully understanding the illustriousness of the present, he cherished it fiercely. Clearly from a time when Jack did not exist, the mechanism was in stark contrast with the rest of his contemporary appearance. However, Jack loved the old watch all the more for it, and always took it out when he had nothing better to do with himself. Automatically, as was the established habit, he began to run his thick fingers over it, feeling all the intricate grooves and lifts.

Noticing something that was from the same era as she, Meredith took delight in the silver and gold watch. "Oh, that is grand," she said, admiring it nostalgically.

"Thank you," Jack said while getting up and holding the pocket watch out for her to hold.

Waving her hand as though she did not need to study the antique any closer, Jack sat back down. "How did a man so young as yourself come across such a watch?"

Smiling widely, Jack proudly said, "It was a gift from my father. It had been a gift to my father as well, when he was my age, from his father."

"Well…" she paused, as though looking for a notion. "Jack, I think it's lovely. It reminds me of when I was a young woman."

At once excited by such a rare opportunity, Jack asked with thinly camouflaged fervor, "Would you care to tell me about when you were a young woman…Meredith?"

Meredith began to look off into the proverbial distance with her mouth opening ever so slightly, but then began shaking her head slowly, "No, Jack. Thank you, but no, I won't bore a person with such tales."

Knowing that to push was both rude and futile, Jack merely nodded with a pleasant expression upon his countenance. And, once again, they sat in a comfortable silence.

After several peaceful moments, Meredith became aware anew of the slender case sitting upon her lap. She held it within her hands and opened it, revealing two medals placed carefully within. "Jack…" she began slowly, "Jack, I think these may have been left in my room by mistake."

Without complete surprise as to why she believed such a thing, Jack inquired, "Why do you think that, Meredith?"

"Well, I was cleaning out my drawers the other day, and I found this case. I wonder if these medals might be left over from another occupant of this room? It says that they are issued to a Corporal Foley, but I don't know such a man. I'm worried that he may be looking for them."

Jack stood up and took the case from Meredith, looking at the medals with visible admiration. "Meredith, do you know what these are?"

"They're medals, Jack. I may be old, but I'm not stupid!" Meredith said with a slight chuckle. She had enjoyed using that particular cliché, given the appropriate opportunity, for some time.

"Of course," Jack replied with usual amusement. "However, these are more than just medals. This," Jack pointed to the medal on the right, "is a Purple Heart. And this," he said as he pointed to the medal on the left, "is a Bronze Star. Both were recently issued to Corporal Foley."

"Well!" Meredith blurted out, plainly impressed. "He sounds like quite a man. We really need to return them to him, he surely must be missing—"

"Corporal Foley wanted you to have them," Jack interrupted with careful gentleness.

Clearly touched, Meredith questioned, "Why in the world would this Corporal Foley want me to have his medals? I imagine that he would want them!"

Returning again to his place on the recliner, Jack confirmed, "Meredith, Corporal Foley is not among us anymore. However, he did, indeed, want you to have those medals." Jack paused as he looked for some semblance of acceptance from Meredith, "And that's why you now have them."

"But I don't even know who this man was! Surely his wife would want them." Once this statement was made, Meredith began to grow thoughtfully concerned. "Oh, he must not have been married...Poor soul," she mumbled as she became lost in thought.

"No, Meredith," Jack gingerly interposed once again without a hint of frustration, "Corporal Foley was married—"

"Mrs. Finch?" A nurse abruptly interrupted as she entered the room. "Sorry to barge in, but it's time for your meds."

"Oh, Barbie-Sue, that's quite all right..." the elder said as she held her hand out for the numerous pills while granting Barbie-Sue a reprieve for disrupting the conversation. After taking the last of the pills, Meredith playfully probed, "Barbie-Sue, you're not married, are you?"

"Yes, ma'am, I am," Barbie-Sue replied to Meredith as she waited for the seasoned woman to finish her glass of milk, a necessary post-cursor to any ingestion of medication for the cranky stomach. "Been married eleven years now."

"Oh!" the slight woman exclaimed. "Well, I think Jack here may be too young for you even if you weren't married!"

Barbie-Sue glanced at Jack, whose face had turned as scarlet as a red pepper, and winked at the younger man. "Yeah, I think he may be a hair too young for an old coot like me!" the dangly nurse voiced with bemusement.

The silver-topped matron instantly began to laugh as she choked out, "Old coot! My foot! You've still got your whole life ahead of you. Your best days are just getting started. Why, I was probably about your age when I met Mr. Finch. He had been back from the war for a few years when we met." It was with this that Meredith began to take on an air of somberness. "I do miss him...Do you know how he died, dear?" Meredith asked Barbie-Sue. After waiting for Barbie-Sue to shake her head several times, Meredith completed, "Mr. Finch died from Emphysema. I knew those things would get him. Of course, we didn't know how bad they were for you back then, but I always guessed that sucking in smoke on a regular basis couldn't be good for the bags. He wouldn't give them up, though. Not even for me..." As her voice trailed off and reverberated against the little room's walls, Meredith again took on the appearance as though she may be reliving a chapter of her long life within her mind.

Having waited several long moments, Barbie-Sue guessed that Meredith was going to remain encapsulated within her thoughts, so she nodded at Jack politely and began to walk out of the room. Suddenly, so suddenly, in fact, that it startled both Barbie-Sue and Jack, Meredith's voice pierced the silence out of nowhere with, "We'll see you later then, Barbie-Sue."

"Yes, ma'am, I'll be back for your bed-time meds."

Without watching Barbie-Sue leave, Meredith began to muse over her thoughts afresh. Although Jack would have gladly given a year of his meager salary to know the reflections that were taking place before him, he felt that it was important to finish the conversation that they were having.

"Meredith," Jack interrupted. After waiting for her to make eye contact with him, he continued, "Would you like to know the story of Corporal Foley?"

Visibly honored to have been the final person chosen to hold Corporal Foley's medals, Meredith answered affirmatively, adding, "So long as you make sure to mention why he has given me the distinction of now owning these medals."

"Of course…" was the quiet reply of the self-proclaimed bookworm. Jack sat back in his chair and, while still holding the esteemed medals, began the story that he knew as well as his own:

"The man we're respectfully calling Corporal Foley was actually known to his hometown of Beaumont, Kansas, as Lawrence Hudkins Foley. He was born on November 24th, 1921, to a family of oil field workers. Even though he was quite gifted in school, he could never have afforded college and so was well on his way to a life of being an oil field worker himself. When he was twenty-one, though, his life as an oil field worker ended when he answered the call, as did so many others his age, and entered the service on July 27th, 1943."

"He was so young!" Meredith exclaimed. "Of course, they all were," she said with remembrance. "They all were…"

After waiting a few moments out of respect to those Meredith was thinking of, Jack continued, "As you know, Meredith, America's involvement in World War II was already established by the time Lawrence joined. Lawrence loved his family passionately and was severely troubled to leave them; however, he had been a man who had honored obligation his entire life, and this was not going to be any different. I'm told that the realization that to protect his country meant, ultimately, to protect his family, was the prevalent reassurance he had in what he was doing. The opportunity to secure a safe future for his loved ones compelled him to believe in the task that he was undertaking. He left a man devoted to his cause.

"Lawrence was sent to Camp Adair, Oregon, where he trained with the Army for one and a half years. Judging from the letters he regularly wrote home, he was incredibly frustrated at being detained so long. He would often write that he felt cowardly that so many men were dying every day while he simply trained for combat. He was growing tired of drilling for a war that he was beginning to fear he would never see."

"Did he ever get to see his family during that time?" Meredith asked.

Nodding, Jack answered, "Yes. I think that they got leave every once in awhile."

With her face brightening, Meredith said, "Ah, yes, I remember joking with my girlfriends about how they spent that time."

Completely understanding her implication, Jack simply continued, flushed, "In the summer of 1944, Lawrence was transferred to Fort Leonardwood, Missouri. He stayed there for what was another agonizing six months, until he was again relocated to Boston, Massachusetts. It was from there that Lawrence was finally going to be sent to the war that was taking place overseas. He left in early December of the same year on the USS Westpoint, a former cruise liner that was being re-utilized."

With her brow furrowed, Meredith declared, "Why, the war was nearly over! That must have been horribly frustrating for him!"

"I think it was," Jack nodded. "He finally made it over, though, after what was a long ride across the ocean. He landed in Marseilles, France, in mid-December. He was a Corporal by that time, assigned to an anti-tank crew in the 276th regiment of HQ Company, 2nd battalion.

"The fighting began immediately, but, according to his letters, so did the camaraderie. I understand that Lawrence was very popular among the men because of his easygoing manner. His letters were often very optimistic, even though he was going through the same hell that everyone else was having to overcome."

"How any of those boys kept their chin up is beyond me," Meredith said in a whisper with a dazed look on her face.

"Lawrence fought his way, along with the rest of the men, north into Eastern France near the Germany/Switzerland border. His letters often wrote about how he lost many friends on a daily basis, and that he could never get used to it. He said that he would mourn for them when he got home, and was frustrated that there just wasn't time to stop and think about them. I'm told that one of his letters said that he felt like if he stopped to mourn for them, then part of him would realize just how random death was over there. He wouldn't let himself think about death; he only wanted to focus on staying alive.

"He helped others stay alive as well," Jack said with a smile. "I heard about a time that the Corporal found a young baby in the rubble of a recently bombed building. The town had been completely evacuated and, for a reason that remains a mystery to this day, the baby had been abandoned."

Aghast, Meredith fought to restrain her voice, "Surely it must have been beyond control. I can't believe any mother would ever willingly leave her child behind! That's terrible! Simply terrible!"

"Well, the baby was fine," Jack reassured Meredith, "and the next sign of civilization was in Gaubiving, the town they were headed to, so Lawrence cared for that baby for three days until they reached their destination. I understand that he got the nickname 'Pops' from his buddies after safely depositing the baby to more conventional caretakers.

"The men were billeted in Gaubiving, France, and stayed there for many days. During this stay, Corporal Foley would often volunteer to go on patrol around the perimeter. No one wanted to patrol, and Corporal Foley's peers all thought that he was surely crazy for always volunteering for the mundane duty. The young Corporal had his reasons, however. Evidently he was so homesick after missing the holidays with his family that going on patrol was the only thing that comforted him. Walking in the darkness with the snow on the ground reminded him of home just enough to help ease his mind, according to a letter he wrote on January 25th.

"As he was patrolling, he spotted a private in a foxhole named Bud Anderson. Bud was the only soldier that Lawrence hadn't gotten to know very well, so he told the private to quit wasting time in that foxhole and assist him with his patrol.

"As the men crunched through the snow in the dark getting to know each other, they thought that they heard incoming artillery. Lawrence hurled Bud to the ground and dove next to the young private. There hadn't been any artillery fired at them, as it turned out, but when they plunged to the ground one of them triggered a trip flare that was set up as a perimeter alert."

"Oh, my..." Meredith whispered as she brought her hand up to her mouth.

Searching the eyes of Meredith, Jack continued as delicately as he could, "The flare hit...It hit Lawrence directly in the face." After a pause to ascertain whether or not this narrative was too much for the dignified woman, Jack quickly felt that it was appropriate to continue. "The flare bounced off of Lawrence, and then hit Private Anderson in the arm as well."

"Those poor young boys!" Meredith cried out vehemently.

"The men in camp came running to the sounds of chaos," Jack continued at Meredith's unspoken behest, "and saw Private Anderson holding Corporal Foley in his arms. With what they saw before them, the men quickly dropped to their knees and said a prayer for the twenty-three year old Corporal. It was in an apple orchard in Gaubiving, France, on January 26th, that Corporal Foley did what so many other men of his generation had nobly done, he gave his life for his country and his family."

"He was only there just over a month..." Meredith uttered to herself, shaking her head in disbelief. "Did he have any loved ones besides his parents?"

"Yes," Jack answered promptly, "he did. He had a son named Ross that was two at the time of his death. He also had a new baby daughter that he had never met. She had been conceived while he was still in the states on leave, as you touched upon earlier. And, of course, he had a wife that he loved more than anything. He wrote letters to her every moment that he had to spare."

Paying heed to her gesture, Jack handed the Purple Heart and the Bronze Star back to Meredith and listened attentively as she inquired, "Who was it then, that first received these beautiful medals on the young man's behalf?"

With rapture immersing Jack's face, he announced, "It was Ross, in fact, who first received the medals that we have before us." Noting the confusion on Meredith's face, Jack continued, "Lawrence—Corporal Foley—did not receive these medals until nearly sixty years after his death. It was Ross, who had no recollection of his father, who began to investigate the circumstances of Corporal Foley's death only a few years ago."

Baffled, Meredith asked, "Ross and his family didn't know the circumstances of the Corporal's sad end?"

"Not exactly," Jack answered. "Bits and pieces, at best. However, for whatever reason, Ross, who was by that time sixty years old, began to voice his passion for knowing more about his father. It was Ross' own son, named after the Corporal, who suggested that Ross become proactive and get online. By 'online,' I mean the Internet. You see, Meredith, the Internet—"

Appalled at Jack's condescending views of her technological savvy, Meredith blurted out, "I know what the Internet is, Jack! I e-mail people all the time!"

"Oh," the educator muttered, a bit hurt that he had never received e-mail from Meredith. "Well, at any rate, Ross and Larry, short for Lawrence, of course," Jack winked to Meredith as he saw that she had reached this conclusion on her own volition and was about to announce as such, "eventually found the web site of the 70th division. This was Corporal Foley's division, known as the Trailblazers. The father and son posted a request that if anyone knew Lawrence Hudkins Foley, his son and grandson would greatly appreciate hearing from them."

"Isn't that remarkable!" commented the up-to-date senior. "I think that the Internet is just magnificent!"

"As I understand," Jack continued with veneration at the old woman's refusal to lag behind, "it was absolutely amazing how quickly the responses came flooding in. Contacts came from Arizona, Oregon, Texas, Idaho, and Florida. Slowly, Ross was able to piece together the exact circumstances of this father's death. Perhaps the greatest information Ross obtained was the fact that his father had not died alone, and that he was given a prayer at the time of his death."

Nodding her head emphatically, Meredith commended, "That was the right thing to do…"

"In fact," continued Jack, "Ross eventually came into contact with Bud Anderson himself, the private that was holding Lawrence after the accident. Private Anderson, now nearly eighty-five, had been under the delusion that he had abandoned Corporal Foley after the flare erupted. For decades, Bud Anderson had been in and out of therapy trying to deal with the guilt that he had felt since 1945. He had apparently gone into shock after the flare hit his arm, nearly severing it and sending him into the hospital for several years. No one had ever told him that he had, in fact, held Corporal Foley as he died while help arrived. He had no recollection of it at all," Jack said while shaking his head sympathetically.

"Fortunately, the peace of mind Bud Anderson had given Ross by making sure his father did not die alone was given back to Bud in the knowledge that he had acted honorably. He couldn't believe that the recollection of his actions had been false for nearly six decades!"

"I'm sure he was perfectly shocked!" Meredith declared.

Jack resumed, "After obtaining all of this information and having spoken with the Corporal's band of brothers, Ross felt that his father deserved the Purple Heart. He became obsessed with the idea and wrote to his local congressman, who was happy to assist Ross in going through the proper channels for such a request. At first, Ross was disheartened by the news that the commissioning of the medal could take years. As you can imagine, Ross felt immense delight when, after just one month, his father was appointed not only the Purple Hearth, but the Bronze Star as well! It had apparently been the quickest securing of medals that his congressman's office had ever seen. It is with the medals that you hold before you that Ross and his family finally felt closure to the death of Corporal Foley."

Meditating deeply upon the story she had just heard, the slight old woman began to close the thin black case that the medals were housed within and placed them on her nightstand. As she slowly executed this act, she knocked some of her medication off of the nightstand and onto the checker-tiled floor. Perceiving Jack's immediate declaration that he'd pick up the expelled vials, Meredith said quietly, "Well, both Corporal Foley and his son sound like wonderful men!"

Feeling a smile form across his face as he reached under Meredith's bed to find the jettisoned containers, Jack finally grabbed hold of them and began to stand back up. As he did so, he noticed through Meredith's view of the parking lot that his parents' car was now parked next to his, and thought that it would be only seconds before they entered Meredith's room.

"Well, Meredith, from what you've told me," Jack affirmed as he placed the Alzheimer's medication back to its assigned place upon the nightstand, "Corporal Foley was a superb man and a loyal, loving husband. As for Ross, well, I think Dad would have made Lawrence proud."

Jack noticed a tear fall from Meredith's eye as she and Corporal Foley's first-born walked into the room.

The Marble Man

The failed author took a sip from his coffee as he pondered over the next line of his story. It was an unusually cool morning for the month of August. So cool, in fact, that the young man sat with his windows open in his little apartment while he worked on what he hoped would be the one to finally make it. Luckily for him, he literally moonlit as an author. His actual profession was that of a teacher at the local high school. But this was summer. And for him, summer meant that teaching was over and writing was the name of the game. It was a perfect situation considering that he was still being paid for the nine months that he had taught.

The local weather lady said that there was an awful storm on the way. Supposedly, it was to arrive shortly after midnight. Considering that it was now three in the morning, he felt sure that the moisture he smelled in the air was as unlikely a sign of things to come as were his chances of getting published.

He put down his coffee and placed his fingers back on the keyboard. He had begun writing this particular tale at eight o'clock. Even with the ensuing dawn of a new day, he was no less blocked now than he had been seven hours prior.

"Mark," he said to the little stature of Mark Twain that he had sitting on his writing desk, "how did you do it?" After several seconds of silence from Mark, the contriver began trying to write again.

Just as he almost had a decent word to type out on the fifth page of what was shaping up to be an awful story, there was a heavy knock on the door to his apartment.

The writer pushed his heart back down his throat as he sat with wide eyes. He didn't even have the nerve to turn and face the door. The only person who ever knocked on his door is his girlfriend, and she'd been asleep in her own home for nearly six hours at that point in time! Other than she, the inadequate author didn't believe anyone had knocked on his door once in the year and a half he'd lived in the humble hole in the wall.

He sat for what seemed decades in silence. Just as he began to believe that he had imagined the horrendous knocking, a single, reverberating crack shook his whole building. This time, more than the amateur's heart jumped as his legs hit the underside of his writing desk, toppling the precious coffee.

He turned and faced the door.

Several more centuries passed as he refused to blink with thunder in his ears.

"Do not make me knock again," a soft, cement voice ravaged from the out-side.

Paying no attention to the coffee spilling onto the cheaply carpeted floor, the scribe stood up from his black, foldout chair and walked through five feet of mud to finally reach the door.

"I'm waiting…" whispered the hollow voice.

Recently having forgotten how to breathe, the young man forced himself to peer breathlessly through the peephole to the outside.

What he saw in a strangely concave fashion was what appeared to be a man wearing a black top hat and a black cloak. The little light posted upon the wall outside of his apartment threw shadows over the figure so that the rest of its appearance was indiscernible.

"I don't know you! I think you've got the wrong place!" the young man cried through the door.

"I do not make mistakes…" was the stone reply.

"I'm calling the police!" whimpered the man as he turned and rushed to his bedroom. He clung to his cell phone as he began to dial 911. He had managed to hit the nine when he realized that he had an uninvited guest standing within his living room.

The phone hitting his bare foot after it had been absent-mindedly dropped caused little pain. The only registered pain was in the young man's temples as his madly pumping blood threatened to burst free like an overflowing dam. Only meters away stood the shape wearing the black cloak and top hat.

"Come closer," the one in black ordered.

"I don't want to…" the young man replied as he vaguely remembered the English language. With thousands of panic-ridden thoughts racing through his mind, the author did not register the thick sheen of sweat oozing from his pores.

The dark being's head was lowered so that the brim of the top hat covered most of its face from view while it rested heavily upon a silver cane that obviously was not needed. Then it spoke, "Patience is a trait for that I am not renowned. I suggest you approach. Quickly."

The room was noticeably several degrees cooler as the terrified author trudged from his bedroom to the living room. As he approached, he hated himself for writing by candlelight. He could not see the foreboding figure very well at all with the wild candle's shadows thrown about the room. He could, however, see his own breath as it exploded from his mouth.

Only a body's length away from the frame standing impossibly next to the author's bookcase alongside his front door, the individual who wore midnight finally lifted his head high enough for the young man to see the countenance. The face looking through him from the depths of opaqueness horrified the writer.

The face seemed to flawlessly be made of gray marble. Its features were perfect. Perfect, and inexplicable. Also preternatural, to the young man's severe discomfort, were the chiseled one's eyes. There were none. Only two, large, barren sockets that seemed to be bottomless pits existed and were fixated upon the drowning author as he choked for air.

Finally, the desolate, cold slab of a voice demanded, "Sit."

Of course, the only movement that the man was aware of was that taking place within his bowels. Any voluntary movement on his part was quite impossible.

Without a hint of agitation, the featureless one lifted the silver cane and used it to guide the useless young man past the little coffee table and onto the synthetic black leather couch.

Head lowered once more, the man of gray rock stood before the tenant within a veil of shrouded blackness. "If I wanted you to be harmed, you would have been so long ago," it said.

Trying desperately to ignore the torturous sweat that was dripping from his forehead and burning his eyes, the author somehow muttered, "I don't have any money."

Could that cement face smile? It came as closely as stone could move before the phantom figure answered, "Your currency is as useless to me as is your body."

The young author shook his head in confusion at the odd statement. "I'm not sure what that means…"

"What that means," it clarified, "is that I do not plunder. I have no need. Do you know what I am?"

Millions of premises dashed though his mind, but the unsuccessful scribe quickly decided that the simplest answer was the best. "No."

Again, a sound of faint rock brushing against rock in what could have been a grin below the brim of that black hat seemed to take place. "I collect souls when they no longer have any terrestrial importance, and then I guide them to the afterward."

Squinting his eyes in disbelief as they began to tear up, the seemingly already defeated author muttered in anguish, "You're the Grim Reaper...Does this mean that I'm dead?"

"No. Any being devoid of life would be incapable of leaking as much fluid as you are presently. I am not the 'Grim Reaper.' That is a creation of those who dabble in your profession."

"Teachers?" the young man questioned.

"Scribes," replied the dark one blandly.

His egocentrism still fully intact, even while nearly frightened to death, the aspiring author began to babble in mock humility, "Well, I'm not really a writer yet. You see, I'm a teacher. I write on the side, but I haven't actually been published."

The young man quickly ceased his stammering when he saw the gloomy figure wave its gloved hand towards the candle, extinguishing it instantly. Now the only light that remained was that which was being illuminated from the computer screen.

Completely engulfed in darkness, the shadow entity spoke almost inaudibly. "You are a poor example of a writer at this stage. However, you have a future in the profession. I am here to warn you."

"What do you mean?" the distressed man asked.

"Your composition will be the death of you. In your future, a reader will murder you over a story written by yourself. I am here to help you avoid the unpleasantness. That is, if you're willing to pay heed. Write no more."

"Why would you warn me of this? I thought that you collected souls," asked the inquisitive and unsettled young man.

"Do you always question what seems to be fortune at your doorstep?"

"When am I going to write this story?"

The young man heard a rustle of rock and cloth as he felt a slight whoosh of frigid air. The light from the computer did nothing to aid his perception of the mysterious visitor. In an instant before his candle caught flame again, the author heard the icy voice lecture: "Time is irrelevant to me."

The living room was once more visible. The top hat and cloak were gone and the thermostat was rising like a geyser. The teacher jumped from his couch and fell into the foldout chair in front of his computer. He quickly erased the rubbish that had been upon his screen. Now with a blank page before him and the thunder and lightening finally having arrived, he wrote the title to the first work he'll have published—"The Marble Man."

Proposing to Krissy

I just asked her to marry me and she's crying hysterically. Ordinarily, this would be sort of expected. After the last twenty-four hours, however, I truthfully have no idea if these are tears of joy, sorrow, anger, horror—you name it. Seriously, though, can you blame her? I really think you'd be crying too.

Of course, you have no idea what I'm talking about, do you? Well, since I'm hanging between nanoseconds here as I wait for the love of my life to kick me to the proverbial curb, I guess I have plenty of time to fill you in. This will enable you to make an informed decision as to whether you think I'll have a fiancée by the end of this tale, or if I'll simply have a broken heart. As I'm sure you're well aware, I think it will be the latter. Of course, I'm a pessimist.

We had planned several months ago to make sure that we go SOMEWHERE for our one-year anniversary. ANYWHERE. As do all of you, I'm sure, we get very stressed out by our jobs and made a solemn vow that we would RELAX on our one-year anniversary regardless of how much work it would take. Yes, that was supposed to be a joke.

Somewhere between the time of planning our vacation and a few weeks ago, we started looking at rings as well. Now, I'm madly in love with Krissy, you must understand that, and as we began to look at rings I had it in mind that I would propose very soon indeed. Coincidentally, I was telling her that I would not propose to her until enough time had elapsed for her to forget the very ring she had decided she wanted. Right, as though that would be possible. At any rate, I thought it was a first-rate deception.

So, with the ring picked out mere weeks before our one-year anniversary, I figured that our big trip would be the perfect time to propose! I'm very obsessive-compulsive once I get an idea in my head, so I immediately started making all the necessary preparations. Before I picked up the ring, however, there was one very important task yet to perform:

"Hello?"

"Mike?"

"Hi, Scott. What's going on?"

"Is Jill around?"

"Sure, let me get her—"

"Actually, could you stay on the phone too? I kind of need to talk with both of you."

"Sure, hold on," Mike said with more than a hint of suspicion.

A few moments that seemed like an eternity passed before:

"Hey, hon! What's going on?"

"Hi, Jill." A deep breath was taken here. "I'm sitting in a parking lot right now because I told Krissy I was going for some gas, so I've got to make this really quick." Oh, no. I just told them that I had to be quick. Keep going, keep going. "Er, anyway, I love your daughter very much, and I was wondering if you'd let me propose to her?" Oh no again. Idiot. Idiot. Idiot.

Long pause. (Or, at least, it felt very long.)

"Scott, every dad dreams of this moment and wants to have the perfect thing to say when it comes along. She's my little girl, and I want you to treat her right. I also have to give you fair warning, you have no idea what you're getting into with this family!"

Thank God. He made a joke. Jokes are good. Jokes make me relax.

"Oh, honey. We consider you one of our kids! We love you just like we love Krissy and Chad. Of course you may propose to her!"

"Thank you so much." Wait, I think I feel my hands again. Okay, I'm breathing. Good. That's good. "Well, let me tell you what I have planned. I drove down to Hawk's Landing the other day and met with the wedding planner—"

"The wedding planner!" Jill choked out. The fear in her voice was nearly tangible.

"No! Not to get married!" Yikes! "I had called her earlier and told her that I wanted to propose to my girlfriend while there and asked her if she had any good ideas. She started rattling off some thoughts and I decided maybe I should just drive down and take a look around."

"What'd you think?" Mike asked.

"At first, I wasn't really happy with it," I answered.

"But you'd already made reservations, hadn't you?" Jill asked.

"Yes, so I was starting to freak out a little. I originally had thought about taking a hike through the woods and asking her at some nice spot."

"And?" Jill asked.

"And Lisa—"

"Who's Lisa?" Mike interrupted.

"Lisa's the wedding planner."

"And she's helping you plan your engagement?"

"Right," I responded.

"Okay," they said in unison.

"So as I was saying, I wanted to find some kind of a brook or meadow or something along a hiking trail and ask there."

"Sound nice!"

"Thanks, Jill, I agree. One small problem—you have to hike ten miles through relatively nothing before you find a pretty spot out there."

"Um, Krissy's not much for the outdoors," Mike offered while trying not to burst out laughing.

"I know! Our canoeing trip last summer where she nearly drowned and I nearly got eaten by a rabbit proved that! Yeah, the woods are out."

I was quite sure I heard muffled laughter on the other end of my cell phone. Quite sure.

"Well, Lisa suggested that I team up with the resort's magician our first night there and work something out during his show in the lounge. I thought that was a bit too much spectacle, as well as far too inviting to the dreaded x-factor."

Oh, you moron. You didn't know the meaning of the word x-factor yet. Foolish fool. Redundant, yes, I know. It's for emphasis. Work with me, please.

"So, did you come up with anything then?" Jill asked.

"In fact, I did." Oh, how naïve I was. Thoughts of self-congratulations were running through my mind before the next statement: "She finally took me out back to check out Lake Green Valley. As we walked to the lake along a paved path, past the outdoor pool, there was a spectacular gazebo not far ahead, at the end of the path, directly overlooking the lake! 'That's it!' I screamed like a little feminine boy. I nearly hugged Lisa I was so happy! To make a long story short," (I know what you're thinking, shame on you), "I worked it out with Lisa that I'll give her a budget to work with and she and her people will decorate the gazebo our second night there while eating in the resort's restaurant. After dinner, I'll take Krissy out to the lake where we will stand in the gazebo garnished with white lights and flowers and I'll get down on one knee and ask her to be my wife. While I'm doing that, Lisa will have a dozen red roses delivered to our room awaiting our return. It will be perfect!"

"That's a lot more than I did…" Mike mumbled.

"It sounds wonderful, Scott! She's going to love it!"

"Thanks! We'll get down there on Friday, the twenty-first. We should get there around six, so we'll have dinner in the resort's restaurant that first night as well, then maybe take a swim in the indoor pool. We'll wake up the next morning and get some breakfast in the restaurant, then hit some great antique stores and grab lunch in Green Valley. Then I figure we'll take a nap or swim some more until dinner. Then, after dinner, the rest of our lives together begin!"

"Scott?"

"Yes, Mike?"

"One thing…"

"What's that?"

"Didn't you tell Kristen before you called us that you were just going for some gas?"

"CRAP!"

And so the next few weeks went by with me an anxious mess until finally the twenty-first crawled along.

The drive to Hawk's Landing right outside of Green Valley was rather uneventful for the first hour. That is, until Krissy asked me if I knew where I was going. This is probably as welcome of a statement to a man as is the offer of a last request for a death-row inmate. Okay, that was a bit of an exaggeration. But seriously, fellas, am I right? Oh, are the married guys too scared to answer? Wimps.

Anyhow, I assured her that I knew where I was going. I told her I was just going to take a bypass to miss the downtown area of Airless Springs. This opened the floodgates to a disagreement that ended in a call to her father to make sure that her (supposedly) navigationally challenged boyfriend was not a complete ignoramus in this regard. Please don't ask me about other regards.

What was the real kicker as she essentially took away my manhood while checking directions with her father is that I had JUST made this trip a few weeks ago when I went to Hawk's Landing to plan our engagement. Of course, I couldn't tell *her* that. The things men must endure in the name of Romance. Don't think I didn't hear that sound, ladies.

So finally we reach Hawk's Landing. The place is as dark as a dog who just ran through tar. That didn't really make any sense, but you get the idea. The resort lights were on, don't misunderstand, but there was no other light anywhere in the parking lot, and keep in mind that we were in the middle of a state park. Somebody didn't even bother to turn the moon on for us. Jeesh!

After stumbling through the darkness that was their parking lot, we wandered into the main lobby. It was just as lovely as the day I had visited several weeks ago. A massive fireplace in the center, a grand piano off to the side, beautiful paintings along the walls—Magnificent!

We approached the front desk to check in. The desk worker quickly got us checked in and even suggested a different room for us on the main floor. She said it had a better view and we'd probably enjoy it more. Marvelous! I instantly took her up on the offer. Have you figured out the problem with this move yet, gentle reader? If not, don't feel bad, it would be nearly five more minutes before I caught on to it myself.

So Krissy and I dragged our luggage not very far at all to the room. We walked in and the room looked just as the other one I had seen a few weeks earli—ahhhhhh, NUTS! It finally registered with me that the room looked familiar because Lisa had shown me a room on the lower level, near the gazebo, and we decided I'd just take that room. Still not seeing the problem, esteemed reader? Well, that's okay. The problem, or x-factor, as some would call it, was that I had arranged for Lisa's people to deliver a dozen roses to our room while we were out at the gazebo. If we change rooms, what if Lisa's people didn't catch on and the roses got delivered to the original room! My perfect plan had been compromised! Calm down, Scott, yes, I can hear you saying it, just let Lisa know that the rooms were changed. Rather simple. Yes, it would have been simple had Lisa worked the weekends, but I was positive I had heard her say she wasn't going to be around that weekend, but not to worry, everything would be prearranged. As long as, that is, NONE OF THE PLANS CHANGED!

Think fast, think fast, think fast.

Nervous walk to the curtain. Quick glance out the window. Nothing but darkness (for the moon was still unplugged, apparently).

"What? This is no good! The view is terrible!" I yelled out.

"Scott, it's dark out, there is no view," Krissy reminded.

"Oh, no," I stumbled out, "I can just tell, we're facing that parking lot! The original room faced Lake Green Valley! I want the other room back!"

"Okay," Krissy agreed rather amiably, "this room smells a little musty anyway."

Hauling the luggage back to the reception desk. A quick explanation to the helpful young lady that I'd like the original room back because it had a view of the lake. A quick explanation from her that it really had more of a view of the putt-putt course than the actual lake. A quick explanation from me that ANY view of the lake was a good one. A quick look from the honest-to-goodness-trying-to-be-helpful-but-ultimately-throwing-the-proverbial-wrench-into-my-plans-reception-girl.

She switched the rooms back. X-factor denied! I'm the man! No more problems, and even if there were, I knew I could handle them. I'm the man? No, trust me, I'm just a little boy. And yes, there were more problems. Many. More. Problems.

A quick drop off of luggage to the room, a quick comment from Krissy that the room smelled kind of musty, then off to the in-house restaurant, the Gennysaekwa.

"Yes," I began, trying to sound like a mix between Bruce Wayne and James Bond, but probably coming our more Gomer Pyle than anything, "reservations for Crawford at 6:30."

"Yes, right this way please."

"You made reservations?" Krissy asked, obviously impressed.

A debonair smile from yours truly, a comment that we had reservations for tomorrow night as well, and then we found ourselves seated.

Several long moments go by. Have you ever noticed that when you have a whole lot of time, you tend to become intensely aware of your surroundings? And how utterly crappy they are?

"What can I get you?" a rather less-than-prim-and-proper waitress asked us in her best smoker's voice.

"A menu would be wonderful..." I mumbled to her.

Do you smell it, dear reader? Yes, that's the smell of an x-factor.

Eventually, two rather greasy, old menus were brought to us. Keep in mind that this is supposed to be a very nice restaurant. At this point I'm scared that if I use the restroom there'll be a glory hole in the stall wall.

"What are you having?" Krissy asked me.

"What the heck, it's our anniversary, I think I'll have the filet mignon!"

"That's not too expensive?" Krissy asked after finding it on the menu.

I began to shake my head "no" and I implored her to order one as well. Yes, they were expensive, but as already noted several times, and feel free to say it with me, it was our anniversary.

Well, I won't bore you with the insanity-inducing details, so allow me to summarize: Salad...bar. Yes, we had a salad bar if we wanted our salad. Not great for the prices they were charging, but not unforgivable either. Dinner was served: Cold vegetables with a film over them. Cold mashed potatoes with no butter or sour cream. Filet mignon that appeared to literally be two flank steaks stacked on top of each other. No, I'm not joking. Yes, I was EXTREMELY pi—, er, upset. Here's the conundrum, fair reader: If I caused a scene and all of these same people were working tomorrow night, I'd compromise the sanctity of my master plan. After all, the restaurant folks were to tip off the rose deliverers when we got up to go for our walk to the gazebo tomorrow night. Ever the politician and avid poker player, I thought I might have to eat it this time (figuratively and literally, now that I think of it) and pretend I liked the meal.

Before we got up to go back to our room, Krissy made a comment that went something like this, "We'll have to cancel the reservations for tomorrow night, I'm never eating here again."

Remember that comment about me being a boy? That comment you just read by Krissy alerted me to the fact that perhaps I'm, indeed, not the man. Perhaps I'm not the slayer of x-factors. Only time will tell, as, if you'll recall, we are living between the nanoseconds of my proposal and her response as I pick you up to speed. Ergo, on with the tale.

After dinner we decided to go for a swim at the indoor pool, after waiting the perfunctory twenty minutes, of course, just in case our mothers are reading this.

Long part of that episode of the story put short, the pool was freezing, people were in the hot tub. Eventually the people got out of the hot tub, we got in, then they came and closed the pool and hot tub.

So, back to the room we went. A brief conversation about dinner. A rather uncompromising statement about never eating in that restaurant again. A bit of a pathetic plea that if you really love me, you'll eat in the restaurant the next night. A rather uncompromising statement about never eating in that restaurant again.

To bed we went. Straight. To. Bed.

I can't speak for her, but I did not sleep well.

It's now a bright new day! I roll over. There's my beautiful girl, the love of my life, hopefully my future wife. Hey, that kind of rhymed, didn't it? A quick shower taken by each of us. A quick comment about eating at the restaurant that night. A rather uncompromising statement about never eating in that restaurant again. A bit of a pathetic plea that if you really love me, you'll eat in the restaurant that night. A rather uncompromising statement about never eating in that restaurant again. A bit of a melodramatic march out of the resort's room with an unnecessary slamming of the door.

Yes, it was your humble narrator who threw the temper tantrum.

So now, dear reader, I found myself in the parking lot, which was clearly lit by the sun (no problems with keeping it working, apparently), and calling her mother on my cell phone to try and figure out how to eradicate this latest x-factor. Aren't these x-factors a pain in the butt? Back to the task at hand, if anyone could help me solve this problem, it'd be Jill.

The phone rings. And rings. And rings.

Guess what? Yes, that's quite right! Jill's not home.

Okay, her mom's not home. Being the man that disintegrates x-factors, I fell back to my next partner in dealing with problems. My mommy.

I got hold of my mom, but the best advice she had was to fall back on the ol' reliable, "If you really love me..." Well, we all know how well that worked, don't we? I explained it to her for us. Mom's final idea was for me to put Krissy on the phone with her, and she'd talk to her woman to woman. I quickly determined that a woman to woman talk with her (hopefully) future mother-in-law was probably not the best course of action when planning to propose within the next nine hours. Mom understood. She was only trying to help, after all.

Back into the resort I went, directly to the front desk.

"Yes, hi. My name's Scott Crawford, I'm proposing to my girlfriend on the gazebo tonight." I waited for the smile and nodding to cease, and then, "Yes, I'm going to need to speak with the manager." The smile quickly dissipated.

A quick request to hold on a moment, a rather anxious holding on for a minute, and then the door to the office swung open. I sure hoped this manager would be of some help. And guess who walked out of that office, honorable reader. Can you guess?

LISA!

Yes, it was true! God didn't hate me after all! Lisa stood before my very eyes! I nearly hugged her I was so elated to see her before me.

"Lisa, I thought you didn't work weekends!"

"No," Lisa responded, "I work until five on Saturday's. What's going on? There's not a problem, is there?"

I could see in her eyes that she knew by my expression that there was a problem. A serious problem. A problem called the Gennysaekwa. I asked her if there was somewhere private that we could talk. She showed me to her office.

Well, after a long explanation of the previous night's meal and its utter repulsiveness, I explained to her that Krissy wanted to eat dinner back in Airless Springs and leave Hawk's Landing as far behind us as we possibly could. Lisa was just mortified with the Gennysaekwa and said she completely understood. She told me that she'd make sure we were not charged for the second night of our reservation at the resort.

Believe it or not, venerable reader, I still hadn't given up hope. I wanted to marry this girl with all my heart, and while I was quickly realizing I was not the terminator of x-factors, I still wasn't going to give up. I asked Lisa if there was any way the gazebo could be ready by, say, three in the afternoon. I told her that we still wanted to grab some lunch in Green Valley, and hit their antique stores. We then were going to come back and maybe I could propose at that time, if the gazebo could be ready in time.

Lisa explained to me that the gazebo would not be a problem, but it wouldn't be dark enough by three for the white lights to show up. She asked me if I could stall Krissy until, oh, around four-thirty.

YIKES!

I commented that I could maybe suggest we open gifts after we go to the antique stores, then go look at the lake. Lisa thought this was a good idea, and I did too, except for the fact that I'd only gotten Krissy a couple CDs to go along with the ring for our anniversary. The only reason I got the CDs was just so I didn't drive down without any visible gifts compared to her twelve for me (yes, dear reader, you're quite astute, a gift for every month we'd been together).

Okay, I figured that it would just make the proposal that much more of a surprise if she thought she only got two CDs for our one-year anniversary. I was praying, at least, that this would be the case.

Lisa assured me that the roses would still be delivered while we were on the gazebo, she gave me a late checkout time so I wouldn't be charged for the second night, and she apologized on behalf of the Gennysaekwa. That Lisa. She was the best. If you ever read this, Lisa, you're the best!

So, back to the room I went. I found Krissy sitting on the couch, watching TV. Her eyes were red, and it was obvious that she'd been crying. Oh, I felt horrible.

Before I could open my mouth to apologize, she immediately told me that she didn't know why it was so important that we eat in that darn restaurant, but if it meant that much to me, she'd do it.

Now, I don't like lying to my Krissy, but with a fairly strong plan B in the works, it was crucial that she not suspect anything. I think she was suspecting that I was going to propose to her in that disaster of a restaurant. So, I had to lie to her. Sorry Mike and Jill, I lied to your daughter.

"Honey," I began, "we don't have to eat there tonight. You see, it was so important to me that we eat there because I was going to have lilies delivered to our table while we ate. They are your favorite flowers, aren't they?"

Krissy ran across the room and gave me a strong hug. "Baby," she began, "you got that upset over lilies? I mean, it's a really sweet idea, but you were going to pay all that money again for a horrible meal over flowers? You're too sweet!"

I'm fairly sure that sweet was a synonym for stupid, in that particular case.

<RIIIIIINNNNNGGGGGGG!>

Oh, no.

The phone.

My cell phone.

I took my cell out of my pocket, and it's Mike. Mike, as in Jill's husband, Krissy's father. I knew the minute I saw his name on my caller ID that he'd seen my number from when I tried to call Jill and wanted to make sure everything was okay.

"Hi, Mike."

"Hi, Scott. I saw you'd called; is everything okay?"

"Oh, right. Yeah, I was just calling to make sure that lilies were Krissy's favorite. It doesn't matter, though, because I think we're going to leave early. We had a horrible dinner last night, and the room smells kind of musty."

"Oh! I think I'm with you. I know you can't talk now, call me later and tell me what's going on."

"Okay, Mike, thanks for calling. Yes, I'll tell her you said 'hi.' Bye-bye."

Yes, I'm going to Hell—I know.

"You went to all that trouble, Scotty, just for flowers?" Krissy asked with her eyes tearing up.

"Yes, but don't you worry about those flowers. I went and talked to the manager and told him that we were irate about our horrible meal. I told him that after we go to the antique stores in Green Valley, we are leaving Hawk's Landing and we will never come back. I also told him that I demanded a late check-out since we're having to change our plans on such late notice due to his establishment."

"Are you serious?" Krissy asked.

"Heck-yes, I am. We'll eat in Airless Springs tonight on our way back home. If my Krissy doesn't want to stay a minute longer in Hawk's Landing, then she's not going to. I told that manager exactly what was on my mind!"

"You're my hero!" she sang as she hugged me again.

Yes, we've already established the fact that I'm going to Hell.

Well, as our nanoseconds are quickly growing to a close, I fear I may have to speed things up. You've been such a good sport so far, I know you're just sticking it out by this point to hear Krissy's response. Trust me, that makes two of us!

At any rate, we left to go to the antique stores in Green Valley. Of course, I spent twenty minutes taking us in the exact opposite direction of Green Valley (I'm going to maintain that this was a ploy to kill time, should she accept my proposal and I reveal all my master deceptions to her). Finally, we got to Green Valley and could not find any of these antique stores we'd heard so much about. While grabbing a quick bite at a certain fast-food place with yellow curves (I wanted to eat at a pizza place to kill time, Krissy thought it'd take too long), we asked someone if they knew of any antique stores in the area. After a loud conversation across the joint with a mother and daughter who, added together, weighted nearly a ton, I'm sure, we felt fairly certain that there were not nearly as many antique stores as we'd heard. Well, we found a few. In our region of the state we call what we found flea markets. Around those parts, they called them antique stores.

Before we left Green Valley I wanted to stop and look at their huge dam that held the water of Lake Green Valley at bay. I really just wanted to kill more time, and we wound up spending a solid ten minutes at the dam. Oh, and I nearly twisted my ankle while walking along the sidewalk. You know, I really HATE x-factors.

We did FINALLY manage to find a decent (and legitimate) antique store, and, thank God, spent nearly an hour in it.

So we got back to the resort at around three-fifteen. I still had nearly an hour and a half to kill. As we walked into the resort, I asked Krissy if she'd like to grab a drink in the resort's lounge. A couple of drinks would probably kill a good forty-five minutes, then we'd open gifts, go for a walk to the gazebo, and we'd be right on time!

Krissy declined on my offer to grab a drink.

XXX-FAAACTOOORS!

To the room we went.

We opened gifts. I played up the fact that I felt really bad she only had two CDs and I had twelve (one for each month, don't forget!) gifts. I told her that the lilies and their delivery were to be part of her gift from me.

She told me that the gifts weren't important, it was just getting to be together on our anniversary, no matter how horrible the resort had been.

I suggested we go for a walk. It was nearly three forty-five by this point. I thought I could take her to the docks first, then work our way back through the resort to the gazebo.

I executed that plan, and it took up a good fifteen minutes. So, almost half an hour too early, we turned back to head for the gazebo. Of course, she had no idea the gazebo was even there; we were supposedly just going for a good view of Lake Green Valley.

Back through the resort we went, past our room (I pretended as though I was going to enter the room, but she reminded me we were going to look at the lake; I really think I could be a secret agent), and headed for the indoor swimming pool. We went through the sliding doors that led to a path headed to the lake, and for the gazebo we were then destined. She didn't know this, of course. I sure did, though. My heart was beating like a jackhammer!

As we walked along the little paved path through some very light trees, we noticed another gazebo to the left.

"Look!" she said. "A gazebo! We'll have to work our way over there after we see what's at the end of this path."

"Good idea!" I said mirthfully.

As we kept walking, we began to notice some lights up ahead in the waning sunlight. Have I mentioned how awesome Lisa was?

"Are those lights?" Krissy asked.

To answer in a word—yes. About twenty feet ahead of the gazebo, Lisa and her people had lined white Christmas lights up along the edges of the path. The path led directly into the gazebo, and the gazebo was draped in white flowers, white Christmas lights, and white lace. This view, coupled with the natural beauty of Lake Green Valley, made for a magnificent sight.

You know what? As I think about it, maybe when these nanoseconds are up, I'll get the answer I wasn't expecting at the beginning of this tale. I need to hurry this up so I can hear what she has to say!

I saw Krissy's eyebrows furrow together and chuckled inaudibly when I heard her say, "It looks like someone's going to have a wedding out here!"

"Maybe we better turn around?" I offered slyly.

Krissy looked at me, and I knew that her Lewis and Clark spirit would never turn back having seen the gazebo. "Heck, no!" she squeaked. "There's nobody around, let's go look at it!"

So onward we walked toward the gazebo that was nearly as beautiful as Krissy herself, and we quickly noticed that there were two chairs set up in the center of the gazebo, facing the lake.

"It's so pretty!" Krissy cried as she looked around. "What do you think it's for?"

I smiled and felt my heart begin to burst it was beating so fast. I started to drop to one knee while taking out the brilliant round ring I had gotten for my brilliant girl and said, "It's for you, Krissy. This is all for you." Now, the following were my exact words, "Krissy, I know this weekend's been a bust, but will you marry me?"

Smooth, I know.

Krissy burst into tears.

And so, dear reader, you're all caught up. Our nanoseconds have drawn to a close and now we finally get to hear the answer that we've been so anxiously waiting for.

I look up into those wonderful eyes of Krissy, and she says, "Yes, of course, I'll marry you!"

TAKE THAT, X-FACTORS!

I spend the next half an hour hugging and kissing Krissy and explaining to her all the plans I had made, all the adjustments I had to make, and how I developed a rather unhealthy loathing of the dreaded x-factor. We have Lisa come out and take our picture in the gorgeous gazebo and we both thank her for her unrelenting work. We then spend several more minutes holding each other and looking out across the lake.

When we return to our room, there sit the dozen roses. Krissy loves them, but not nearly as much as I love her.

We do still leave Hawk's Landing early, as our readjusted plans dictated, but now we're not so sure we'd never be back. We wind up having dinner on the way home with Krissy's folks in Airless Springs, where they live, and we have a good laugh about all the escapades that had taken place. We call my mom and dad from the dinner table to let them know that even without the woman to woman talk, things still turned out great.

So I guess that's the end of my story about proposing to Krissy. God knows there's plenty I left out, but you got the most important details. We'll be married in a few months, and I love her more with every day that goes by. If I had one piece of advice for you, it'd be to never give up on love, no matter how rough things get. Never let those darn x-factors get the upper hand!

The Bridewell House

Speeding through the dark town in the old Mustang, the newly defeated teammates thought little of their customary loss as they listened to the booming music. Even the primordial roar of the car's engine was a weak challenger to the music, and so the four boys were happily forced to yell and laugh over the clamor.

Steve suddenly realized that his forever-lucky friend, Breaks, was shouting at the top of his lungs for the car to pull over. Once Steve had successfully crossed the 7th Street railroad tracks, he accommodated his old friend.

"What's up?" Mark questioned from his place in the back seat with Richie.

"Look over there," Breaks demanded.

The other three boys refused to acknowledge Breaks' request because they knew, as did all of Kithlessville, what lay to the east after crossing the 7th street tracks.

"So?" Steve asked in mock confidence after turning down the music and glancing into his rearview mirror. Although he knew what had suddenly taken such a hold of Breaks' interest, he asked anyway, "What are we looking at?"

"The Bridewell House," Breaks answered without trepidation.

Three backyards to the right was the location of the Bridewell House. Its backyard, like all the houses along King Street, fed directly into the railroad tracks. However, unlike the other houses along King Street, it was completely dark with not a body stirring within.

More than a little unnerved, as any sensible person would be, Richie questioned, "What about the Bridewell House?"

"Let's check it out," replied the fortuitous boy with eyebrows raised as he made eye contact with his uncomfortable teammates. He relished the slight groan he heard come from within their souls.

The Bridewell House was one of those dwellings of lore that every small town has as routinely as a barbershop and an apothecary. Sadly, however, the circumstances leading to the inauspicious legend of the Bridewell House were firmly rooted in tragic reality.

Decades ago, when Kithlessville actually had a winning football season, a catastrophic accident occurred upon the railroad tracks that bisect 7th street, the very tracks that the young men just passed over. Difficult as it is to describe, a school bus from the town's elementary school was approaching the tracks at the same moment as the impending passing of a freight train. Of course, the warning lights were flashing, signaling 7th Street's automobilists to halt. Leading the commute on 7th, heading north, was "Rocket" Pabst. "Rocket" was a nickname given to Charles Pabst in jest of his extraordinary reluctance to go over 15 mph while driving in town. Many felt that this character trait made him the perfect choice to transport the town's future before and after school. They were horrifyingly wrong.

Understand that it was no fault of Rocket's. An autopsy revealed that he had been a narcoleptic. No one realized that Rocket's famed napping was much, much more than just an amusing trait of an old, seemingly tired man.

Although the train was well within the parameters of the legal speed for a locomotive passing through town, the dead-center impact was horrendous. The bus was mauled several hundred feet before the train came to a stop. When the screaming of child and machine finally came to an end, both were parallel with the Bridewell's backyard.

Once they were loosened from the ravages of the bus that was fused to the train, the emergency personal had little choice with where to place the bodies of the children. There was little choice in the matter because several more tracks lay on one side of the catastrophe, and backyards lay on the other. Therefore, the bodies of twenty-four little boys and fourteen little girls were placed in the nearest yard, that of the Bridewells.

No town should ever have to go through what Kithlessville went through that day.

It wasn't long before the Bridewells moved out of their home, relocating to Texas. They claimed, understandably so, that they could no longer look at their backyard without seeing the desecrated children of that day.

Because this was an otherwise industrious era for Kithlessville, a new family from out of town moved into the Bridewell House. They soon moved out without an explanation to anyone. This began a trend that lasted for fifteen years. After a decade and a half had elapsed, the town finally left the Bridewell

House alone, and it seemed perfectly content with the decision. It has stood devoid of life at 55 East King Street ever since.

"Maybe we should take Richie toilet papering instead," Steve apprehensively replied to Breaks' request of "checking out" the Bridewell House. Richie instantly became excited at the prospect of his idea from earlier on how to spend Friday night apparently being re-opened.

After noting a brief comment of approval from Richie, Breaks retorted, "What are you guys, scared?"

"Yeah, Breaks, we're afraid of some old house. Give me a break, um, Breaks," Mark stumbled out, obviously aware of his pun far too late.

Triumphantly, Breaks said, "Well then, let's go have a look."

After taking a quick right onto King Street, the boys found themselves pulling up alongside the dilapidated old house. Steve cut the engine and the silence screamed at them to leave immediately without looking back.

"Look, guys, why don't we just head downtown; you know that the rest of the guys will be there. Maybe we'll even see Anita and you can try to get back on her good side after ditching her tonight," pled the uneasy Richie.

Laughing, Breaks retorted, "She's not mad! Why would she be mad? I told her something else came up."

The rest of the winless Kithlessville Cougars within the Mustang shook their heads in disbelief to one another. After all, there *was* a reason that they called him "Breaks."

"Let's head on in," continued the all-state fullback.

"Um, look, Breaks, I'm with Richie on this one," began Steve. "I really don't think this is a great idea."

With anger growing stronger by the instant, Mark raged, "He's totally playing us, don't you realize that? He doesn't want to go in there any more than we do; he's bluffing!"

Blue eyes suddenly open wide, Breaks irately rebutted, "You think I'm hustling you, Botrip? I'll go in there right now, alone if I have to. Heck, I'll even stay there the whole night just to prove you wrong!"

"Whatever," Mark dismissed.

"Guys, maybe we should calm down a little," Richie mumbled.

"No way, Naderi!" Breaks yelled as his adrenaline mounted. "In fact, I'll give each of you ten bucks if I can't last the whole night in that place."

"You're both being stupid—" Steve began.

"Tell you what, Breaks," Mark blurted out, "we'll each give you twenty bucks if you *do* last the night in there!"

Aghast, Richie appealed, "Hey, you're betting *my* money. That's not cool."

Lifting his square, stubble ridden chin high, Breaks proclaimed, "You're on, Mark!"

"Chris, come on, this is pointless," Steve begged.

Taking hold of his friend's shoulder with his powerful left hand, Breaks whistled, "This'll be the easiest money I've ever made. Easier than the time I ate that earthworm for fifty bucks at football practice. You remember that?" After waiting for Steve to grin with his nodding, Breaks continued, "You're not going to hold out on the Chris "Breaks" Ralson fun fund, are you, buddy?"

Taking a deep breath and then exhaling a slow sigh, Steve shook his head while answering, "If you want to do this, I'm in. Richie?" Looking behind him and waiting for Richie to hesitantly nod in the affirmative, Steve finished, "Let's do it."

The friends got out of the car and stood before the Bridewell House. They noticed that they saw every feature of it perfectly within the bright moonlight. Every crack of the paint, every window that was broken, and every missing shingle they mentally catalogued. They treaded up the walk between the jungle of grass. Three of them swore that they heard a warning as they stepped onto the creaking porch. The fourth claimed that it was just their stomach rolling because they were about to soil themselves.

Exchanging hesitant glances to one another and then to the doorknob of the abandoned dwelling and back to each other again, Breaks finally chuckled a bit and made contact with the house that didn't want to be entered.

The door to the Bridewell House was easy enough to enter. All Breaks had to do was turn the knob and push. As he did so, years of dust was pushed aside by the moaning door. Because there were no curtains or shades, the moonlight provided enough light for the boys to see by fairly well.

They noticed the dust lying as a sheen of gray snow on the floor after having collected undisturbed for decades. There was very little furniture in the deteriorated, rather eerie house, only an end table or two that must have been deemed unworthy for retention, as well as an old rotary phone still plugged into a useless jack in the corner of the entry hall. As the athletes walked by, it inexplicably rang thirty-eight times.

It took an eternity for the ringing to complete, and as the phone shrieked at the boys to get out, they simply stood inertly with their hearts firing rapidly.

Finally, the ringing died. Fighting against their instinct to turn and run, thanks to Breaks encouragement, Richie, Mark, and Steve instead continued to walk through the musty house. They listened neurotically to the weeping of a floor that was no longer accustomed to bearing human weight. Soon, they entered what must have been the family room and noticed a staircase leading upwards. A large, rectangular window across from the staircase gave a perfect view of the moonlit backyard and the railroad tracks.

"This is it," Breaks mused gleefully, "I guess I'll see you guys tomorrow!"

"Wait a minute," Mark contended in the illuminated family room, choking slightly on the particles of dust that he and his friends sent airborne with each movement while trying very hard not to let his voice quiver. "How do we know that you're not going to walk home as soon as we leave? You can come back in the morning before we get here and collect sixty bucks!"

"What do you want to do, glue me to the floor!" Breaks sarcastically responded.

Not really knowing why he said it, Steve whispered, "I've got jumper cable in my car."

Richie cocked his head to the side and gazed at Steve with narrowed eyes, "You want to tie him up with jumper cable?"

"That's perfect!" Breaks happily joined in. "You can tie me to these rungs," he said while quickly running his finger along them and producing a sound that could cause insomnia. "That way you'll know that I can't cheat you out of your money! Go get the cable, Steve!"

Steve turned and jogged out of the family room to his car while feeling not quite himself and oblivious to the disapproving glares of Richie and Mark.

Shaking his head, Mark finally said, "Breaks, this is crazy. You've got me. If you're bluffing, you win. We're not tying you up in this freak palace. I'm getting the creeps just standing here. You win, okay? We need to get out of here. You win..."

"I haven't won yet, Marky," the muscular athlete sang. "But I will when you come back tomorrow morning." Motioning to the quickly returned cable-wielding Steve, he quipped, "Let's go, bud. Wrap those things around me."

Realizing that Breaks was unreasonable at moments such as this, Mark said, "Let me at least get you one of those end tables to sit on if you insist on this idiocy." With that, Mark began to leave the room, then abruptly stopped as he hit the doorway.

Richie and Steve quickly gawked at Mark, apprehensive due to the sudden halt in fluid movement. "Richie," Mark began with a hint of shame in his voice, "come with me. I don't want to be alone in this place."

"CHICKEN!" yelled the exhilarated Breaks. "You are such a coward, you can't even walk a few steps by yourself?"

When Richie and Mark returned with the abandoned furniture, they saw that Steve had already secured Breaks to the rungs of the banister. At Breaks' order, Steve pulled hard on the fullback to verify that the cable had no give at all. It did not. They placed the end table under the dark-haired young man and he took a seat with a wide smile.

"Listen, boys," he said after shifting around a bit to get as comfortable as he could with tight jumper cable binding him, "I want you to go straight home. Don't go downtown or anything, because you know that one of you will tell the rest of the team what's going on, and then, when you come back here tomorrow and see me with a smile on my face and sixty dollars richer, you'll think someone came and set me free overnight. Deal?"

"It's past eleven already," Steve said after lighting up his digital watch, "I don't have a choice. My parents are going to kill me." At the mention of that word, Steve, Richie, and Mark felt the room grew very cold and he instantly regretted having said it in a place like this. Breaks, of course, seemed to notice nothing but his own delight.

Throwing off Steve's comment, Mark attempted one last appeal with Breaks, "This is not a good idea…Chris, are you sure you want to do this?"

"I'll be fine!" Breaks laughed. "What could happen to me? No one knows I'm here but you guys! Nothing's going to come and get me if nobody knows I'm here! You all seriously need to relax."

Mark dropped his head and mumbled against his will, "You've got a deal then. We'll see you in the morning…"

"I'll pick Richie and Mark up around seven, then we'll be right over. Okay, Chris?" Steve asked with eyebrows raised in distress.

"Why don't you make it noon?" Breaks teased. "I'd hate for you guys to miss your Saturday morning cartoons!"

And with that, the boys began to walk out of the family room while listening uncertainly to Breaks' good-natured jabs at their bravery. Following Richie and Mark, Steve took a last look and saw Breaks smiling at him, white teeth shining brightly in the moonlight amidst all the dust beneath him.

They left their friend within the Bridewell House.

＊

"So you left him alone that night. What next?" asks the blonde-haired man.

"Kyle, you realize that we were found completely innocent of any wrongdoing, right?" Steve responds with stone in his voice.

"Yes, Steve, I do realize that…You were saying?" the man named Kyle prods.

Irritated, Steve begins, "Kyle—or should it be Officer Cooper?"

"Kyle's fine, Steve. I'm off duty. Otherwise I wouldn't have this in my hand," Kyle says as he lifts a bottle of beer up from the table.

Nodding to himself in embarrassment, Steve mutters, "Of course. How stupid of me…Kyle, why are you asking me about all of this? It's old news. Everybody knows the story. What's your interest?"

Before Kyle can answer, a woman that Steve doesn't recognize approaches the officer and begins to whisper in his ear. Steve takes a sip of his whisky and cola as he waits for the interruption to end. He knew it was a mistake to come. Mark and Richie had been smart enough to avoid Kithlessville from the moment that they graduated. Now with Mark studying to be an eye surgeon and Richie already a wealthy dot-commer, they didn't want to dig up any old bones. Steve had been optimistic. Life was going so well for him, he didn't think that there could be any harm in attending his fifth-year reunion.

He was wrong. It was obvious from the beginning that no one was going to have anything to do with him. He'd been sitting alone at the bar chosen for his class' rendezvous since the moment that he had arrived. Kyle Cooper, the least likely candidate in his youth to become a police officer in Kithlessville, was the only one willing to converse with Steve. Unfortunately, Steve had already realized that it was not out of friendliness.

Steve cannot understand his classmates' frigid reception towards him. His last year and a half at Kithlessville High School had been uncomfortable, but never had people acted so blatantly loathsome towards him. He begins to desperately wish that he had gone to visit Richie as his old friend had begged him to do instead of coming back to his hometown.

"When I hear it all, all of it, from you, I'll tell you what my interest is," Kyle answers as the woman walks away from the police officer, but not without a dirty look shot at Steve. "I know you don't want to talk about it, Steve, but I need to hear it from you—personally."

Steve takes a deep sigh. He doesn't really trust Kyle. He never has. But, Steve has been drinking alone long enough by this point to feel that talking to someone about an uncomfortable topic is better than talking to no one at all, so he continues:

"I picked up Richie and Mark the next morning and we drove across town to the Bridewell House. It was just after six in the morning. I don't think any of us slept a wink that night. But, with the early morning signs of daylight, our fears subsided and our spirits rose.

"I think we all felt like we had been pretty silly for worrying about Chris. I mean, after all, *he* was the one who wanted to spend the night tied to the rungs of a staircase banister!

"As we drove, we actually began to laugh at how Chris had revealed us all to be nothing more than scared little boys. Now, of course, I wish he had been one as well. We all had our money out and ready to go, and we all agreed that Chris had most certainly earned it this time."

"Right," Kyle interrupted, "Get to the part where you see him."

Slightly unhinged by Kyle's rudeness, Steve refuses to cut his story short, "You said you wanted the personal version of what happened, or did I misunderstand?"

"Don't get cocky, Walls," Kyle grunts with eyes barely more than gleaming slits, "You may be a big shot college teacher now—"

"Graduate student with an assistantship," Steve interrupts coolly with his chin lowered and his eyes raised.

"Whatever," the dismissive officer responds. "Just get to when you saw Chris."

"In a moment," Steve reassures. "We once again walked up those steps onto the porch of the house. This time, however, it looked like nothing more than an abandoned building in the early light. And, thankfully, we heard no more warnings from it. In fact, we were already yelling to Chris, calling him 'The Man' and other such names, when we pushed on the door. Our rejuvenated spirits disappeared as it didn't open nearly as easily as it had the night before."

Eyebrows furrowed, Kyle asks with his head slightly cocked to the side, "Why's that?"

After sipping from a drink that does nothing to quell his ever-growing torment, Steve takes a deep breath and says, "The door was blocked from the inside. It took Mark and I both pushing while Richie turned the old knob to get it to open enough for us to slide through. Once through the door, we turned as gray as the foot of dust piled along the borders of the rooms within the house. This dust was blocking the door from within the house!

"Kyle, it was disturbing," Steve utters with a far away look on his face. "While looking at the dust piled up so unnaturally, I began to feel a sort of primal fear within myself. I had to force myself not to scream, abandon my friends, and sprint back to my own house! There was not one speck of dust within the interiors of those hardwood floors. They had been wiped clean. It's just like centrifugal force had bled the dust to the edges."

"Is that possible?" Kyle asks.

Although Steve gives no verbal response, Kyle ascertains from the other man the answer. Steve then continues, "As I fought against running away, Richie was already sprinting to the family room, howling out our friend's name. I took off to the family room also, with Mark behind me. I quickly overtook Richie—"

"You were the tailback," Kyle interrupts.

"Right," Steve answers without interest. "I passed by Richie and beat him into the family room. He was right behind me. I remember hearing his scream when we saw what was before us. Unlike Richie, I no longer had a voice to scream."

"Chris?" Kyle asks.

"Chris…" Steve whispers. "Chris…I'm so sorry." Tears begin to fall from Steve's eyes as the off-duty officer shoves him a napkin.

"What next?" Kyle prompts.

After taking a moment, Steve resumes, "Richie and I were frozen solid, but Mark ran to Chris without a second's hesitation. Even then, I think he had a doctor in him…I felt a hand push me from behind. It was Richie inciting me to move forward. I looked at my friend still held captive by the rungs of that staircase as I approached him step by step. I couldn't believe what I was seeing.

"Chris was trapped by my jumper cables just as we had left him, still sitting on the end table. He was staring out the window into the backyard without blinking. A very slight stream of drool was stretched from the corner of his mouth to his thigh, unbroken.

"This alone had turned my stomach to stone, but it was not what was causing my blood to race."

Steve takes yet another sip of his drink as he tries to maintain his composure and says with difficulty, "Chris…his hair had turned completely white. It was completely…white."

Kyle searches, "What happened?"

"Chris hadn't said a word," Steve answered. "Mark was trying to untie him while wailing for Richie and I to help him. He had managed to get the jumpers unhooked as we stood in front of Chris, and, once freed, he immediately reeled forward and fell onto Richie. Both tumbled to the ground. Understandably, Richie began screaming again.

"I grabbed onto Chris and pulled him up. It must have been pure adrenaline; I never could have picked him up under normal circumstances without getting any leverage. I threw his arm around my neck and propped him up while Mark helped Richie to his feet. We were all looking around the room and pleading with Chris to tell us what had happened.

"The only response we got from him was a whisper into my ear to get him out of that house. I took off in a dead sprint, dragging Chris next to me with Mark and Richie close behind.

"Once we got to my car outside the house, out into the sunlight, we asked Chris again if he was all right. He mumbled nearly inaudibly that he was fine, to take him home.

"Mark settled Chris into the passenger seat and then crawled into the back with Richie, and then I left a set of tire tracks in front of that house that were there for the rest of my days in Kithlessville!"

"They're still there," Kyle interposes, "although time should have erased them years ago."

"I can't say I'm surprised..."

"Go on; what happened then?" Kyle interrogates.

"As we got farther away from the house, we all got to feeling a little better. It was obvious, though, that Chris was not improving whatsoever. We began to joke with him, trying to get some semblance of reassurance from him. He wouldn't have any part of it.

"We finally pulled up into his driveway, behind his old RX7, and began to ask him if he needed any help getting into his house. He was already out of my car and walking up his driveway before we could finish. Finally, in one last desperate attempt to see if our friend was okay, I yelled, 'Hey, Breaks, what about your sixty bucks?' He didn't even turn around as he entered his house."

Squinting at Steve as he takes another gulp from his drink, Kyle goads, "That's it?"

"That's it, Kyle," Steve answers. "You know as much as I do from that point on. Of course, the minute his parents laid eyes on him, the police were at my door, as well as Mark's and Richie's. Although Chris wasn't breathing a word to anyone, we gave every last detail of everything *we* knew. Unfortunately, the only one who really knows what happened to Chris is Chris, and he hasn't spoken unnecessarily to anyone since the morning we freed him from those jumper cables."

"He was never the same..." Kyle contemplates.

"No," Steve says as his voice begins to tremble, "he quit the football team, broke up with his girlfriend, and dropped out of high school. He moved out of his parents' home and took up work on the river. He didn't have a thing to do with anyone from that morning on. He wouldn't even respond when Richie,

Mark, and I would try to contact him. It's almost as though part of him died that night, and I'm afraid that we killed him."

It is with this that Steve finally breaks down and begins to sob uncontrollably.

"No, Steve, you boys didn't kill Chris Ralson. That's the only thing that I know for a fact," Kyle sighs.

With tears rolling down his face, Steve whimpers, "What?"

Taking a long drink, finishing off the beer, Kyle finally asks, "Do you have any suspicions as to what happened at the Bridewell House that night?"

Finally controlled to a faint degree, Steve shakily returns, "No, not really. I mean, we all have our theories, I guess..."

"Tell me," Kyle demands.

"Well, Richie won't talk about it. Once the police cleared us of any wrongdoing, Richie never spoke a word of it again. Mark and I talked about it quite often, however. We still do. Mark's studies in medicine over the years have led him to the idea that Chris went through some kind of shock that night. He says that any shock severe enough can cause a person's hair to go stark white. Mark maintains that once we left, Chris began to freak out. It's his belief that Chris basically had an anxiety attack for five and a half hours. The part of his explanation that Mark can't explain, however, is the cause of that dust piled up along the walls."

"And you believe?" Kyle begins.

With a cloudy veil suddenly covering his eyes, Steve says, "I think that whatever moved that dust and made that phone ring turned our friend's hair white that night."

"That's not telling me much, Steve," Kyle states impatiently.

"Why are we talking about all of this all over again, Kyle?" Steve restlessly asks.

"Everything I've told you can be found on public record, and it's certainly in your police files."

"I was hoping for a lead..." responds the officer vaguely.

Stunned, Steve responds with, "A lead? What are you talking about?"

Barely audible, Kyle answers, "Chris has gone missing."

"Chris has been missing since his junior year in high school," Steve sarcastically notes in a desperate attempt to hide his growing terror. "I think he likes it that way."

Shaking his head, obviously disturbed, "No, Steve, no. He's gone completely missing. He stopped showing up for work, stopped paying what few bills he was responsible for; he's gone. I've been assigned to his case."

"You have no idea…what's happened to him?" asks the graduate student with his tremulous voice returning. The primal fear he felt the morning that they freed Chris from the Bridewell House was returning as well. Sweat begins to seep from his forehead.

"No. We have evidence. What we don't have is an explanation," Kyle answers.

"What…" Steve pauses as he tries to control his voice and his stomach. "What evidence?"

"We found his Mazda parked outside the Bridewell House," Kyle says with cement in his voice. Steve's heart instantly plummets to his ankles as his shirt sticks to his back.

"Why was it there?" Steve whispers.

"I don't know," Kyle responds, he himself sounding unnerved. "We went inside the Bridewell House and found a pair of size thirteen shoeprints in some pretty deep dust. We followed them to an end table at the foot of the staircase."

"And?" Steve prods involuntarily, feeling as though he's about to pass out.

"They stopped at the foot of the staircase…facing the window."

Trees

The breeze was crisp, but even before she opened her eyes its caress was exquisite. The corner of her mouth rose nearly imperceptibly; however, to call it a smile would be a gross overstatement. With a deep sigh, she opened her eyes. She saw trees.

To be more exact, she saw a multitude of trees swaying back and forth along with the sun winking at her through their gaps. Its warm light felt very good on her nose and cheeks. That smile again nearly reached fruition.

It reminds me of the first time I met Lance, she thought to herself as she watched the underside of the treetops rock serenely from side to side, as though enjoying some easy-listening music.

As effortlessly as a lover's hand slides into that of her soul mate, the trees above her melted into one single tree. She no longer saw what was truly before her vision, but instead was now traveling back through time…

"What's he doing up there?" she asked the young man next to her as they looked up at a bawling child.

"He's stuck, I guess," the man said as he rubbed the back of his head, an attribute that would forever signify simultaneous distress and concern.

"I can see he's stuck," she said with a tone of rudeness that she instantly regretted.

She turned to look at the young man with apology in her eyes but never upon her lips. Her eyes met the young man's and she saw the loveliest shade of brown on this side of the Atlantic. Not only were his eyes magnificent, in her humble opinion, but the rest of his countenance was quite pleasing to her as well, even that slightly crooked nose of his. She imagined upon seeing it that he must be a star athlete and broke it while scoring the winning point. Fate had been far too unstrung for her to be disappointed by the time she discovered that he had actually broken it due to a picture from above his headboard falling upon him while he slept.

By the way he was smiling at her and moving his mouth with only squeaks escaping, she felt that he must have been feeling the same about her. Perhaps the little chicken pox scar above her left eye was as charming to him as his crooked nose was to her.

They stared at each other until the irrational screams above their heads brought them back to the situation at hand.

"Okay," he said to her. "He can't be more than five years old."

"And?" she answered, failing to see his point.

"Well, I'm saying that he probably doesn't weigh more than forty or fifty pounds."

"*And?*" she reiterated. *Cute, but not too much going on upstairs*, she thought to herself. She had yet to discover that when at his most brilliant, he seemed his most ignorant.

"I'm saying that I can climb up and get him," he answered with a far away voice while eyeing the child. It was obvious that he was working out the appropriate calculations of weight versus mass versus tree.

Definitely not too much going on upstairs, she thought. "Are you crazy? What if you drop him? Why don't we just call the fire department or go door to door or something?"

"Look at his hysterics," the young man demanded. Her eyes lifted from those milk chocolate eyes of his to the less appealing wailing child up in the treetop. She could see that the little boy was shaking and beginning to shift around while nestled on the limb. "He could fall out any time! While we wait for the rescue people, he could splat!"

Well, he and I have about the same level of sensitivity. "Maybe I could go for help and you could just keep an eye on him?"

She suddenly heard a yelp and an unnatural rustle of leaves. She immediately looked away from the young man next to her and up to the little boy on the limb. Only he was no longer on the limb. He was plummeting towards her!

She felt a thin but strong hand gently brush her aside and watched this lanky man catch a child falling from the sky. The little boy instantly quit howling as though shocked he hadn't hit the ground. She was shocked as well, to be very honest.

"So, what's your name?" the young man asked her while holding the child in his arms, as though catching babies from treetops was the most normal occurrence imaginable.

She smiled as she answered, "Susan."

The image of his crooked nose and brown eyes dissipated as she returned to the present and saw her contemporaneous treetops once more. However, just as on that day, a smile formed bright and wide across her face. That's when the terror returned.

She had no idea how long she had been out, but the cracking of dried blood upon her cheek caused by her big smile was not a good indication. She instantaneously lifted her left wrist over her face, blocking out the serenity above. The watch's face, along with her own, she assumed, was cracked and it was no longer running.

"Nine-fourteen," she said to herself miserably as she read what the last tick of her wristwatch had been.

Susan knew that her race began at six after nine. She had been making fantastic time considering that she was now a fifty-two-year-old woman running down a trail upon Crestfallen Mountain. It was impossible for her to determine how much time had gone by and how much time she now had.

He was depending on her.

She sat up, wanting to move much more quickly than she actually did, and looked at the culprit. There it was. The autumn leaves had camouflaged a stone that was barely lifted out of the ground from her. Susan saw the stone five feet behind her current position and realized that she had gone on quite a flight.

How much damage had been done, though? It didn't matter. Only one thing mattered to her at this moment as she rolled over onto her knees. She paid no attention to the fact that holes, leaves, dirt, and blood were in those knees, and she stood up. Fire raced along her kneecaps, arced through her spine, and finally settled within the base of her neck. She began to trot along the path once more, this time paying heed to the menacing bumps she saw ahead of her.

The rigidity of her body slowly went away as she picked up speed down the meager grade of the small mountain. She felt the remaining dried blood that had not flaked off beginning to run again as it mixed with her sweat. Even in the brisk air, sweat was now seeping from her forehead, under arms, and back. Physical exercise had never caused her to sweat much. It still didn't. But stress? Anxiety? Those had never failed to open the floodgates.

God, please let him be okay, she pleaded within her mind.

She knew they should have brought the cell phone! Lance wanted no part of that, however. "We're going out into nature, Susan," he'd said with feigned patronization. "How can we enjoy our hike if Amber's calling us to tell us about her latest boyfriend?"

Amber, of course, was their only daughter who was a sophomore at college. Lance had been severely agitated by the number of boyfriends she was going through since her arrival at the university. "It's just a phase, honey. She's figuring out the type of man that she wants to settle down with," Susan had once told Lance. That seemed to make Lance feel a little better about his daughter's relations. Of course, she had only said that to put Lance's mind at ease. Susan decided that Amber was not too old for a little talking to and it would be very soon. Every time she called Amber's dorm room on Saturday mornings her roommate said that she was out jogging. Amber's only allergy was physical activity. Out jogging—her foot!

Thank goodness Susan herself had been a runner even before she had met Lance. In fact, that's what she had been doing when she saw the forever-gangly love of her life staring up into that tree during her junior year in high school. Even so, she hadn't run in years. She'd meant to start up again, but she could never find the motivation. She had found motivation this Sunday morning.

We were about a mile and a half away, she estimated. *I should be getting close.*

Finally, Susan broke free from the forest at the little mountain's base and raced past their Envoy, through the parking lot, and directly to the pay phone. She knew better than to try the doors to the office of the mountain's maintenance people. It was, after all, Sunday. In these parts, only the work that was absolutely necessary was done on a Sunday.

The phone was in her hand and up to her ear within a heartbeat. Just as quickly, she dropped it as searing pain flashed through the right side of her skull. Even so, her right hand immediately groped for the phone again as her left hand pounded out three numbers.

"I have an emergency!" Susan screamed in panic at the voice that answered. After a few agonizing minutes of describing Lance's exact location, Susan slammed down the phone and sprinted past their Envoy once more and into the waiting jaws of the forest.

Now I know why he wouldn't leave that child alone, she contemplated as she listened to the leaves crunch beneath her with each stride. *I never should have left him! What could I do? We had to get help! Oh, God. Please let him be okay. I can't take losing him, too! Not Brett and Lance both, God. Please, not both of them.*

Brett had been their only son. When he was twenty-three, he had been engaged to a young woman that Lance and Susan had considered a Godsend to their troubled son. A life of drugs, alcohol, rehab, and relapse seemed a thing of the past once Lori had shined her light upon Brett's troubled soul. When she died of cancer, though, at the impossible age of twenty-five, their son's soul died with her. Brett reverted back to that dark addict once more and overdosed within three weeks of Lori's death. Even under the careful watch of professionals, their son had found a way.

Susan, with Lance's help, had found the strength to fight through that. Just as Lance caught babies falling from trees, he also caught her each and every time she needed him most. Now, the one time he needed her to catch him...

Finally, after many heart-breaking minutes of racing back up the path, Susan came to the area where the forest began to give way to rock. She jumped up the little slabs of stone until she came to the treacherous hiking. The rock began to get very slippery from years of the elements wearing away at it. She fought to keep her balance as she trotted as quickly as she dared. She went higher and higher, her quadriceps burning with each lunge, up the rock.

Finally, she came to the ledge.

There was a sign posted at the ledge of the twenty-nine foot drop. It warned against standing too closely to it. Folks tended to have an affinity for peering over this ledge at every opportunity. Unfortunately, most folks were also accustomed to some sort of guardrail to protect them. The minute they looked down, most of them experienced vertigo, and right over the edge they went. Lance had once told Susan that thirty-seven people had died at that very spot since they started keeping count in 1952.

"Nature doesn't care about your safety," Lance had often told Amber and Brett as children when they came to this very spot on each of their numerous hikes. "When you're out here, you're on Nature's terms—"

"—and Nature doesn't give second chances," the children would finish for him.

"That's right," he would always say, convinced that he was teaching his children to beware the perils of the world.

Susan dropped to her stomach to avoid dizziness and started to look over the ledge.

Within the nanoseconds before her eyes moved from the stone beneath her to the pit below, the horrendous sequence of events that led to her present crisis flashed through her mind for the billionth time since its original execution.

"Let me give you a hand," Lance had said to her with his back to the ledge.

"I'm fine, Lance," Susan answered as she brushed past him and began lunging up the narrow ramp of rock that led to a plateau above.

"I know you think you're okay, Suze, but you're wearing those darn running shoes! On this type of rock, you're risking your life in those. You need some good hiking boots."

"Lance, I'm comfortable in my running shoes. A snake has never bitten me, I've never turned an ankle, and I've never even gotten poison ivy! I've been hiking with you on this mountain since we were both seventeen, and I've been doing it in running shoes the whole time."

Then, Susan slipped.

She began sliding down the rock ramp and fell backward.

Of course, Lance caught her. She felt his strong hands latch onto her beneath her underarms as her momentum forced him to backpedal down the stone ramp. But then he suddenly released his grasp on her and let her fall right to her rear on the hard stone.

"Thanks a lot, Lance! Why'd you drop me?" she asked as she turned and looked up to see that crooked nose.

No Lance.

Where Lance should have been, she saw only the trees.

Susan shook her head as the latest replay of that awful event ended and she returned to the present. How much time had elapsed since the dreadful accident? She had no way of telling.

She held her breath as she lay upon her stomach and looked down twenty-nine feet to see Lance lying upon his back with both legs bent at unnatural angles. Susan began to whimper as she saw his face covered in blood with one arm resting on his chest and the other pinned beneath him.

A minute amount of dust turned to mud as Susan's salty tears dropped to the stone ledge beneath her. She had wanted to stay with him, but he had convinced her to go for help. He was a dead man if she didn't get him help, he had said so in much gentler terms.

He was lying so still now. After the fall, he had been squirming about, as though he could pop right up after a twenty-nine foot plummet. Now he was still. Far too still.

"Lance!" she yelled down to her beloved, scarcely registering the anguish of the voice echoing her call.

No response.

"Lance! Oh, God! Lance, answer me! The rescue workers are coming, baby! They said they could repel down to you and hoist you out of there! Lance! Please answer me! Help's coming, baby! Help's coming!"

"L-Look up, Su-Suze..." a very weak and feeble voice called up to Susan. Susan breathed a sigh of blessed relief upon hearing his voice and looked up to see the underside of the trees above them. Once again, the sun was peeking at them through the limbs. "It's...It's like when we first m-met," Lance finished as he began to choke a little.

"I know, honey. It's like when you caught that little boy. I remember," Susan called down between tears.

"I r-," Lance began to cough and choke again as he looked up into Susan's eyes twenty-nine feet above him from the stone pit, and then continued, "I remember it perfectly. Y-You're as beautiful now as you were then."

The tears were uncontrollable now. "Why'd you catch me, Lance? Why didn't you just let me fall on my rump?"

"You could have gotten hurt," Lance answered innocently.

"You're always catching people, Lance," Susan cried while stretching out her hand to her husband. "You're always catching people, but no one ever catches you!"

With this, she began to wail in misery.

Susan continued to sob without restraint as she saw Lance grimace in pain while he stretched his hand out to her as well. "You caught me the day I met you," he said.

"You didn't fall," Susan garbled with exhaustion between tears.

"Yes, I did," Lance answered, his white teeth gleaming from within a frame of scarlet.

"Lance," Susan cried out as though tormented beyond her boundaries of sanity, "you did not fall when you caught that child!"

"I fell in love."

Susan dropped her chin to the stone and stared deep into those dark brown eyes, inexplicably growing calm.

"I fell in love," Lance continued, "and you caught my heart."

"I love you," Susan said to her husband gently.

"I love you, baby," he answered.

Several long moments went by as they reached to one another with their wedding rings reflecting the sun's light peeking through the trees, when Lance finally took a deep breath and said, "Look over you shoulder, honey!"

Susan turned around with unimaginable relief as she expected to see the rescue workers. Her heart broke all over again when she saw no one.

She turned back to Lance and said, "Sweetie, there's nothing there. What do you see?"

Lance answered simply, "Brett."

Initially, Susan thought that Lance was simply hallucinating. Upon peering into his deep eyes, however, she quickly realized this was not the case. She felt her throat close up as she wept, "Will you tell him that I love him?"

"H-He hears you, baby. He says he loves you, too, and that he's sorry. Lori's with him. They're happy, Suze. They look happy."

"Don't go, Lance," Susan cried softly with her eyes closed.

In return, Susan heard only the peaceful rustle of the trees.

Freedom's Resurrection

: from the Chronicles of Purgatory Station

It was early evening and Franklin Trover was looking very forward to Sophie's meatloaf for dinner. He loved her meatloaf. So much so, in fact, that he even momentarily considered closing up shop a bit early if it meant digging into the meatloaf sooner. However, Franklin's father hadn't closed early during the twenty-one years of Franklin's life before he took over the shop, and he wasn't about to be the one to break that streak. Trover's Fine Literature remained open until its posted closing, as it always had.

If Franklin had closed his doors early, it would have been the greatest unknown regret of his life, and his brother's.

The familiar jingle of a bell older than most of his patrons signaled the arrival of what Franklin postulated would be just that. The well-read store-owner looked up from his ever-present book and nodded at the young man that entered.

Franklin was accustomed to people wandering about his store rather aimlessly, especially around closing time when many of them were just an hour or so off work. Franklin once stayed open well past nine at night, but the city was now far too dangerous for that. Now it was door locked, gates shut no later than six-thirty.

He could always tell who the nomads were. They'd come in with a look on their faces that Franklin always interpreted as wanting something more from life than sitting behind a computer. They'd ask the storekeeper what he recommended after drifting through the shelves for twenty minutes or so. The conscientious booklover would suggest whatever title he thought would best help them find what they were looking for in life, and they'd almost always buy it, and then they'd be off to take hold of their destiny. That, or else to continue on in their mediocrity.

This one was different. Different by a long shot. When the mysterious figure walked in, he acted as though the sheer number of volumes that awaited him was shocking. Franklin was, well, frankly, surprised at his unusual customer's child-like wonderment as he began to pull books off of the shelves and leaf through them rather sporadically.

As Franklin took stock of the young man, he realized that his routine alertness was not present. When you own your own shop in a city such as this, it's a matter of survival to remain cautionary with everyone and anyone that enters your store. The patron before Franklin should not have been an exception to the rule. It was, after all, obvious that the young man had come across his clothing through rather non-conventional means. His shirt was far too tight, his pants were gargantuan in the waist, his shoes did not match, and it appeared as though the haggard, though handsome, man had not bathed in days. The only thing about the shopper that seemed to be in good shape was a large black satchel thrown over his right shoulder. Of course, this did not include the unlikely consumer himself. He was in excellent condition. Franklin assumed he must be a down on his luck athlete of some sort, for his body was heavily muscled, and Franklin could see from across the shop that he must have been well over six feet tall. Considering his own slender, short frame, as stated earlier, Franklin should have been more alert. This city has never been a nice place, but even it had gone from bad, to worse, to finally whatever is worse than worse. Considering its lackluster history, however, this truly should not have been surprising to its denizens.

At any rate, if you'd seen the young man's face, you would have felt no cause for alarm as well.

Finally, after almost forty-five minutes of the young man devouring books unsystematically, Franklin remembered Sophie's meatloaf and recalled that he had to close in a few minutes.

"Young man," he called from his stool behind the decades-old register, "I surely hate to cut your shopping short, but I'll be closing up soon..."

Franklin felt his heart skip a beat as the tall, lean, muscular man turned his ice-blue eyes to him for the first time. They put Franklin at ease, yet demanded respect from him at the exact same moment.

"Will you be here tomorrow, sir?" the stranger inquired.

Franklin was touched by the man's politeness, but noticed that "sir" was spoken in a manner that seemed to be as customary as folks saying "hello" when they picked up a ringing telephone.

"Yes, I'll be open tomorrow. I'm open everyday of the week but for Sunday. Sunday's reserved for my boss."

"You're not 'Trover' then, sir?" the customer asked with genuine interest.

"No, I'm Trover," Franklin chuckled, "but being an owner of your own business doesn't mean you don't answer to someone else."

"Who do you answer to, sir, if my asking is permissible."

"Well, my boy," Franklin began with a sincere smile, "if you're made of flesh and blood, then you answer to the CEO of the sky, whether you want to admit it or not."

Franklin watched as the dark-headed man nodded while seemingly not to understand.

"So you know my name, youngster, mind if I ask you yours?" Trover began with a grin that he hoped would set the man at ease. He felt a connection to this stranger. Why?

Franklin watched the powerful figure glance to a row of books so quickly that it was nearly imperceptible, and then felt his heart plummet when he heard, "Sir, my name is Hemmingway. Allen Hemmingway, sir." Franklin fought against allowing his disappointment to show. How can one trust a man who will not give his real name?

"So, Mr. Hemmingway," Franklin continued while striving to maintain his cheery disposition, "can I help you find anything before I close?"

From across the room, Franklin watched the young man's sculpted shoulders slump as he slowly shook his head. Allen looked up at Franklin almost with hope after gazing down at the floor with his piercing blue eyes, but then looked back down at the floor once again in despair. He finally drew in a breath as though he were about to speak, but instead chose to only lift his chin back up. He nodded once, and then began to walk toward the door.

"Where are you going, Mr. Hemmingway?" Franklin called out at the last possible moment before the stranger left his bookstore forever.

Allen turned his gaze back to Franklin, seemed to calculate the best possible response, then gave up and mumbled, "I don't know, sir."

"Do you have somewhere you're staying in the city?" Franklin asked.

"No, sir."

"Do you have anyone you can call?"

"No, sir."

"Do you know where your next meal's coming from?"

"No, sir."

"Do you like meatloaf?"

"Sir?"

***

The next morning Franklin walked into Carmah's Cup, located directly next door to his shop, and approached the register. This was the first time in eleven years, the first time since his brother, Walter, had died, that he was not actually tending his store during operating hours.

He saw Julie standing in the back making some simple pastries when he caught the corner of her eye and grinned to himself as she nearly fell over.

"Franklin! Did the store burn down?" Julie cried out in complete honesty.

"No, Julie, the store's fine," Franklin's grizzled laughter erupted.

"Then, what are you doing here?" she asked as she wiped the flour from her hands and left the kitchen. "Nick will be down in a few minutes; he'll bring you your usual six forty-five coffee. Is everything okay?"

"Yes," Franklin confirmed with a smile. His pearl-white mustache lifted up delightfully as he did so. Franklin was in the habit of opening his store at six-fifteen in the morning. He found that he could draw a lot of pre-workday business between then and nine if he did so. He always attempted not to bother questioning the ethics of the people who bought books from him before they went into work, for he knew what he'd do to that type of an employee. Of course, an employee is something he never had the luxury or bankroll to worry over. "Everything's fine," Franklin continued. "I've got somebody watching the register for me."

Julie's rich, smooth voice burst forth with, "Since when do you let Sophie watch the register?"

"Ha! Since never! That woman is the best cook I've ever met, and the best woman since my Mary, but I wouldn't trust her to make change from a penny."

"So, who's the mystery helper, then?" Julie asked as she began to pour Franklin's black coffee into a cup.

"Name's Hemmingway," Franklin snorted.

Julie handed Franklin his steaming coffee from behind her counter and asked cynically, "Does he have a first name, or is it the obvious one?"

"No, it's not the obvious one. He says it's Allen," Franklin answered.

"You don't believe him?" she interrogated as she watched the white-haired, still very lean man sip his plain coffee.

Franklin placed his cup down onto the perfectly clean counter and took on a dreamy look as he asked rhetorically, "Is it possible to know that someone is lying to you, yet trust him completely?"

"What time is it?" a cracking voice interrupted them from the apartment above.

"Twenty 'till," Julie yelled back up the stairs. The hard working brunette never would have done this had any other customers been in the shop, but Franklin was like family to the Carmahs. "Don't worry about taking Franklin's coffee to him, he's standing right across from me."

"What! Did his shop burn down?" the ultra-squeaky voice called down in complete genuineness.

Franklin exchanged a grin with the lovely, curly-haired Julie and then heard her return, "No, he's found help."

There was a sudden barrage of thumps, and before Julie and Franklin knew it, Nick had arrived from above.

"You found help?" Nick appealed in disbelief.

Franklin picked his coffee back up and then mumbled out, "Of sorts," before he took a deeply satisfying sip.

It was at that exact moment that a very modern buzz exploded and alerted Julie that a new patron had arrived. Nick, Franklin, and Julie all turned their heads to see a gigantic blonde-haired man with a dark complexion enter the shop. He held a newspaper under his arm, had the left side of his collar turned up and the right side turned down, and did not so much as nod at them as he sat in a cushioned chair to their left.

Julie smiled at the man and sang to him that she'd be right with him.

"You better get moving," Julie prompted Nick. "You don't want to be late for school."

Julie and Franklin watched as the pimply faced, red-haired boy said his good-byes to them and then bounced out the door. He moved with the exuberance of youth, but it was apparent to both of them that there weighed a very heavy burden upon the boy's heart. It was the same burden that Franklin knew Julie bore.

"It's a fine thing that you're doing…" Franklin offered to Julie as he reached out and touched her red, dry hands.

"I wish I could do more," she responded. "He's actually a Godsend to me. I could never keep up with the evening business if it weren't for him. He waits on tables for me, cleans the bathroom, and even takes out the trash. He does anything I ask of him. Just like he did for Trent."

"Trent was his hero," Franklin said with a solid voice. "Trent was a hero to everyone in this neighborhood."

Franklin kept his hand on Julie's and pressed it even more gently as he noticed her eyes welling up.

"Well, just because Trent's gone, that doesn't mean that Nick isn't still my family. With no real family left of his own, I'm all he has."

"We," Franklin corrected in a very serious voice, "are all he has. And we will be all he needs for the rest of his life. Trent was like a son to me, just like you're the closest thing to a daughter I'll ever have. That makes Nick like a son to me as well. As long as I'm alive, Julie, you won't have to take care of that boy on your own. I swear that to you and Trent both."

Julie slowly walked around the corner of her front counter and met Franklin in route for a deep hug.

Franklin didn't notice the blonde man scowl at them.

***

"Would you like some coffee?" Franklin asked Allen as he re-entered Trover's Fine Literature.

"Yes, sir," Allen answered. Franklin noticed that Allen was in the exact spot behind the register that he had been at when Franklin stepped out, still standing perfectly erect. That had been almost twenty-minutes ago!

"How do you take it?" Franklin asked without really listening for an answer as he tossed down several packets of creamer and sugar. His hazel eyes lit up when he heard Allen comment that he takes it black, and Franklin gushed, "A man after my own heart!"

Then Allen did something that Franklin had not seen him do yet…Allen let out a little chuckle.

When he saw Franklin look up at him with a smile, Allen offered a wide smile back to the older man. Like everything else about Allen, his teeth were perfect.

"I sold a book," Allen announced.

"Really. Did you do it the way I told you?"

"Yes, sir. Precisely," Allen returned without a hint of arrogance.

"Good. You're a fast learner," Franklin praised, "I can tell that about you. How are those clothes working out?"

Allen took a quick glance down at himself and was pleased to see a plaid shirt, a loose tie, a gray vest, and a dark brown pair of pants. "They're very good, sir. It is nice to be wearing clean clothes again."

Franklin stood with surprising comfort on the customer side of his register and watched as Allen took a long swig from his coffee. He knew Allen was about his brother's size. He never understood why he had saved all of Walter's clothes in his old room upstairs, but now he was glad that he had. Heck, Allen now had himself a whole wardrobe, so long as he didn't mind what would politely be referred to as "vintage" clothing.

"They're a tad out of fashion," Franklin apologized.

"Fashion is of no consequence to me, sir. I'm grateful for your kindness. That being said, sir, I shouldn't intrude upon you any longer. Thank you for your hospitality."

Franklin was stunned as he saw Allen pick up that black satchel from behind the counter, shake his hand, and then begin to walk past him.

"Now wait just a minute, son," Franklin blurted out. "You didn't have anywhere to go last night, what's changed between then and now?"

Allen stopped as he stood before the door and confessed, "Last night I needed rest. You gave me what I needed most after my long journey. You've also given me shelter, food, clothes; I can ask no more of you."

"You've been on the run, haven't you, son?" Franklin finally asked with his voice barely audible.

He was not given an answer.

"I don't know what you're running from, but there's a reason you came to my shop. What is it?"

He was not given an answer.

"You don't know, do you?"

He was not given an answer.

"But I do," Franklin said at last.

"Sir?" Allen almost cried out. Franklin could see the millions of questions behind the eyes of the young man, but he was far too disciplined to ask them.

"Come have a seat, please," the older man prompted as he motioned for Allen to join him at one of the reading tables within the shop. He was pleased to see Allen do so without hesitation.

Once they both got settled, each took a single pull from his coffee, almost in total unison. Franklin finally began, "My brother, Walter, told me long ago that one day a man would walk into my store without a clue as to what he was doing there. Walter made me promise that whether he was still alive or not, I would take that man in with no questions asked and treat him as though he were family."

Franklin noticed a spasm in Allen's throat at the mention of his last word.

He continued, "He didn't give me any way of recognizing this man. He just told me that he'd be the only man I ever felt I could trust completely. He said I wouldn't know this man from any other, but that the trust would be there, like a lighthouse to a lost ship, if I paraphrase correctly. I think you're that man, Allen. Are you?"

Franklin was not surprised to see the tall man's head drop between stalwart shoulders in response to his question.

"What's your real name, son?" Franklin asked pointedly.

"I don't have one..." a shamed voice from below answered.

***

Julie heard the buzz of her door opening and left her pastries to approach the front register. As she walked from the kitchen, she noticed that several of her mid-morning customers needed their cups refilled, including that strange blonde man. He made her uncomfortable in a way she had rarely experienced. Yet he was the portrait of civility when she would cautiously refill his coffee. How many hours until Nick got back from school, anyway?

She was quickly shocked out of her ponders as she saw a very handsome, broad-shouldered man with a tiny waist approaching her.

"Can I help you?" she asked the stranger while fighting not to stare at his ocean-like eyes.

"Yes, ma'am," the tall man answered. "Franklin brought me some coffee from here a few hours ago. I wondered if I might have another cup, please?"

"YOU'RE the help Franklin had this morning?" Julie stammered in disbelief.

"Yes, ma'am."

Ma'am? Ma'am? Julie didn't think she'd been called "ma'am" during her entire life. "You look like you might be a bit younger than me, but I don't think I'm old enough to be called 'ma'am' just yet," she chided with a smile. "Call me Julie."

A flash of perfectly white teeth that lit up his whole face, and then, "Yes, Julie. Thank you. I'm Allen."

"Hemmingway, right?" Julie grilled with a wink.

Allen shifted uneasily from foot to foot and seemed at a loss when Julie eventually offered, "So, is Franklin giving you a coffee break?"

"He relieved me from duty for the duration of the day, ma—er, Julie."

"You mean he gave you the rest of the day off," Julie said with a nod. Her brown eyes seemed to be deeper than the depths of space to Allen. He found himself involuntarily peering into them.

"Yes."

"You're military," she deducted kindly, but sharply. "Don't bother to argue, I know the way you all talk. My husband is, too."

"Your husband is military?" Allen asked with unmistakable curiosity.

Julie finished pouring what she could only presume was the wish of Allen—black coffee, the Franklin Special—and handed the Styrofoam cup to him with, "*Was*, I should say. He *was* military. He died six weeks ago."

No longer able to meet the chiseled face before him, Allen averted his eyes and whispered his condolences to her. He noticed her head drop only for a second, and then it was right back up again. "Ulrakistan?" he probed almost inaudibly, already knowing the answer.

"Yes," Julie answered with her shoulders nearly slumping. "Some kids caught them off guard. It's funny, Trent never would have shot a kid, no matter what the child's intention. He always told me that if he had to defy direct orders to keep from killing a child, he would, no matter what the outcome. He never had to make that decision, though," she said with a sigh. "They never saw it coming, from what I've been told."

Now lifting his eyes to the ceiling fan above him, Allen questioned more to himself than to Julie, "But is that the right decision? To go against a direct order?"

"I think so," Julie replied after a moment's contemplation. "Yes, I think so. No matter what the order, if you can't live with yourself afterwards, well, I guess someone would have to decide that for himself. I wish Trent would have at least been given the chance to make that decision." Allen heard her voice crack, he saw her eyes become flooded, but not a single tear fell.

"You're being very strong for him," Allen validated while staring into the deep, dark brown of his coffee. He endeavored to ignore the maddeningly sweet aroma of her perfume.

"He made me promise, just in case," her voice trailed off.

Allen's voice suddenly became very deep and authoritative and Julie could not help but meet his gaze as he established, "Julie, I'm sorry for your loss. Without men like Trent, this nation could not be the light of hope that I know it is."

"Thank you, Allen. But it's not your fault that Trent died. It's war. Until the war is over, we're going to lose more 'Trents' than we can bear."

Allen winced at the words "it's not your fault." Once more, he could not bear to look into the face that he now regarded as total beauty, and then mumbled that he'd better get back to the shop.

"Why?" Julie asked.

"Ma—Julie?"

"Why do you need to get back to the shop? Franklin gave you the afternoon off, remember?"

Julie could see that Allen was growing more distressed by the second. She'd seen that same look from people who felt as though they were in the wrong when they truly were not. Julie knew that if she didn't mend this accidentally and mysteriously broken fence right now, Allen would never feel comfortable around her again.

"Judging from that bag of newly bought toiletries," she began as she leaned over the counter and pointed down to the sack next to Allen's feet, "I'd guess that we're going to be seeing more of each other."

"Yes," Allen answered in agony.

Why was he so uncomfortable all of a sudden? Julie could not understand. "Does this mean you're staying in Walter's old room?"

"Did you know him?" Allen suddenly expulsed in bona fide interest, despite his uneasiness.

"No, he died before Trent and I met. Trent knew him though, always thought the world of him. Are those his clothes?" Julie asked as she looked Allen over. She could smell the mothballs on him and knew they were Walter's clothes without having to ask, but anything to keep the conversation rolling.

"Out of fashion?" Allen grinned as he slowly became more relaxed.

"Tremendously, but on you, they look debonair," she answered with good nature.

And with that, a bond was formed. Could it now ever be broken?

Allen looked around him and offered, "You look very busy, would you like some help?"

"How much do you charge?" Julie smiled.

"One cup of coffee," Allen returned.

"Deal!" Julie laughed out.

***

Later that night, Franklin knocked on the door that was once Walter's room. Now it belonged to Allen for as long as he wished it. Franklin heard a strained call through the closed door to enter, and so he did just that. The white-topped old man was amazed.

He was met with a bed that had been perfectly made, clothes that had been neatly arranged in the closet that had no doors, and several toiletry items arranged methodically upon the oak dresser. He also saw Allen engaged in a set of push-ups that were taking place nearly too fast for his aging eyes to follow.

"Just a second, sir," Allen gasped between pants.

Franklin sat down on the edge of the bed, careful not to crease any of the covers, for while he was not a neat freak, his brother had been. The younger of the two brothers had long ago learned how to adapt in Walter-territory. He watched the statue-like man finish his set and push himself right up to his feet with no aid from the legs.

"You keep in shape," Franklin commented as he observed the sweat ring around the old Harvard shirt that Allen wore. He deduced that this was not the only set of exercises that Allen had completed before the shopkeeper's entrance.

"I try, sir," Allen responded before picking up a neatly folded towel from the rocking chair in the corner of the room.

"Is the room okay? Sorry there's no television. I could pick one up for you, if you'd like. I know a guy down the street who'd sell me one cheap," Franklin offered while watching Allen grin at him.

"No, thank you, sir. I don't watch television. If I did want one, I'd acquire it on my own. You and Ms. Sophie have done quite enough for me already."

"I'm sorry I can't pay you, Allen," Franklin groaned remorsefully.

"Sir, offering me meals, room, clothes, and board in exchange for my work in your bookstore is beyond generous. For me to accept or expect anything more would be an act of crime on my part."

Franklin stood up and adjusted his navy robe a bit as he did so. Allen sat down in the chair. The two studied each other for several long moments.

"You remind me of my brother in so many ways," Franklin whispered.

"Was he a good man?" Allen questioned.

"He was a great man," Franklin answered immediately.

"You both owned the store?"

Franklin let out a hearty laugh and responded with, "Goodness, no! He was a G-Man—"

"Sir?" Allen interrupted in confusion.

"Oh, right," Franklin remembered, "that's not such a common term any more. He was a government agent. They plucked him up as soon as he graduated," Franklin paused a moment and pointed to Allen's shirt, "and he then went to work for them for years."

Allen leaned forward in his chair and asked with anticipation, "What was his duty?"

Franklin grunted heavily as he lowered to his knees and slowly propped himself down so that his belly was nearly touching the floor. Allen was amused to see the old man begin to do a few pushups of his own as he replied, "I don't know his specific duty. He said it was confidential. He was some kind of a scientist/psychologist, I know that much. I heard him talking in his sleep once on my way to the john, kept shouting out something about a map."

At this Allen's eyes grew to the size of softballs.

"How did he escape the position?" Allen demanded.

"He got mauled by some kind of a dog he was experimenting on. Darn thing put him in the hospital for six months. I didn't even know he'd been hurt!" Franklin cried out as Allen counted his fourteenth pushup. "He lost a lot of vision in his left eye and didn't have great use of his left hand any longer, so I guess the government let him go. Can't say for sure, he just showed up one day in the shop and asked if he could have his old room back."

"You both grew up here?" Allen asked.

"Yep. Dad owned this place my entire life and we all lived right here, above the store. It's pretty common for folks who own a business in Old Downtown to live above it. Julie and Nick do the same, next door."

"You mean Julie still does and Trent did before he died," Allen erroneously corrected.

"You've met Julie?" Franklin asked with his narrow eyebrows lifted.

"Yes, I got some coffee after I picked up some items and then assisted her with the shop until her regular help arrived. She's a very strong woman," Allen remarked in admiration.

Was it only admiration, or something more? Neither Allen nor Franklin knew the answer to that for sure.

"Nick's not her employee, Allen! Nick's her brother-in-law! The boy came to live with Julie and Trent after his parents died in a subway accident. He was only there for about a year before Trent got shipped off to Ulrakistan. It's just he and Julie now."

Franklin finally wore out after doing twenty-five pushups, so Allen helped the impressively fit bookseller up from the floor.

"Poor Trent. A good man. We don't have many of those, especially here in Purgatory Station. God rest his soul, God rest his soul," Franklin uttered as he walked over to the chair and used Allen's towel.

Allen reflected as he seemed to have finally solved a riddle and asserted, "The CEO of the sky—correct, sir?"

Franklin laughed and nodded his head while dabbing the sweat from it.

"You a religious man, Allen?" Franklin asked while folding the towel back neatly the way he had found it.

Allen's response was simply, "One nation under God, sir."

"Yes, I figured that much where you're concerned, but do you practice religion?" Franklin chortled.

Allen paused for several moments, as though once again searching for an appropriate rejoinder. Franklin could see that he seemed to have catalogs of things to say, volumes of yearnings to express, but all he heard Allen reply with was, "No, sir. I do not practice any religion to speak of, sir."

Franklin contemplated as he gazed past Allen and then said, "I've got to get to bed, Sophie can't fall asleep without me next to her, but…" Franklin walked past Allen to the nightstand next to his bed. "Walter left you a gift, something he knew you'd want."

Allen stared in disbelief as Franklin pulled out the Holy Bible from a drawer and handed it to him. Allen held it in his palms without knowing what to do, so Franklin opened it for him.

Inside the front cover read, "To the man I knew would come. For the man I knew I could place my trust. Believe in what you read, as I believed in you. Sincerely, Walter Trover."

When Allen lifted his eyes from the inscription, he saw Franklin beginning to shut his door. He heard, "You know to shake the handle on the crapper from last night's adventure, and try to get some sleep tonight."

Franklin winked at Allen and then shut his door.

Allen read ardently until sleep overtook him.

***

"The usual?" Julie asked as she saw Franklin walk into Carmah's Cup, an occurrence that she still was having trouble getting adjusted to.

"You know it," Franklin answered as he approached the front register. He noticed that peculiar blonde-headed man in the corner of the shop once again reading a paper and drinking a cup of coffee. Other than he and this man, the shop was empty. "Is Nick sleeping in?"

"Yeah, it being Saturday and all, I figured I should let the kid sleep in for a little bit. I read that growing boys need lots of sleep so they can adjust to their growth," Julie answered.

"Boy's growing like a weed…" Franklin affirmed while taking his coffee from Julie and leaning on her counter.

"Well, it doesn't help that he stays up all night reading. He can't get enough of this city's freaks. We're the only city in the nation that seems to have a stock-pile of these weirdoes, and Nick won't rest until he knows everything there is to know about each and every one of them," Julie groaned in dismay.

Franklin responded with, "Oh, it's perfectly healthy, Julie. I was the same way. Heck, I think I knew more about Billy the Kid, Calamity Jane, Al Capone, Doc Holiday, Bugsy Malone, and that sort than the best scholars in the country! Even as a grown man, when the Nocturnal Knight first showed up on the scene a few decades ago, I read every news article and book on him I could find! We're always attracted to the unknown and the fantastic. If it weren't this, Nick would be obsessed with UFOs, or ghosts, or whatever. Besides, you know his number-one hero is Trent. Nick's firmly rooted in normal life; don't you worry those curls of yours about it."

"Well, lately all he can talk about is that government character that's gone missing. It worries me, Franklin, that he seems more concerned for the loss of that guy than for his own brother!"

Franklin couldn't help but notice the ears of the blonde man in the corner jerk just a little at the mention of "that government character." Did it mean anything? Probably not. Nick wasn't the only person in the nation to wonder what in the world happened to its only government-sanctioned Colossal.

"He knows that his brother is gone forever, Julie," Franklin consoled with his hand on her shoulder. "We should both hope that his number-two hero resurfaces for the boy's peace of mind. Imagine if he lost both of his heroes within the span of two months…"

Julie whispered something in agreement. She then said she had to get back to making pastries.

"Would you like some help?" Franklin asked her.

"Don't you have to get back to the shop?" Julie asked with total innocence.

"I've got Allen watching it for me. That boy's a workaholic if I've ever seen one! By the time I woke up at five-thirty this morning, he'd already fixed the toilet that's been plaguing Sophie and me for the last few years," Franklin stopped and began to laugh. "When I asked him how he knew how to do it, he said that he had a basic knowledge of plumbing."

"Really? Maybe he could come fix the sink in our bathroom for us?" Julie mused excitedly.

"He could do more than that. After I showered and got dressed, I walked past his bedroom on the way downstairs and saw that he had installed those closet doors I've had off to the side for twenty years! When I got downstairs and found him opening the shop up a little early, I asked him how he knew how to install them. He said that he had a basic knowledge of carpentry! Isn't that a hoot? I swear, if Sophie didn't do all the cooking for us, I bet the boy would fire up the stove and then say he had a basic knowledge of the culinary arts!"

Julie giggled at this as they entered the kitchen and began working on the pastries. After fifteen minutes of Franklin proving he had no basic knowledge of anything involving pastries, Julie commented that maybe he should go get Sophie to come help them.

It was at that exact moment that they heard a single, thunderous gunshot.

The blonde man in the corner was nowhere to be seen.

***

Allen was busily reading the gift that Walter had left him when he heard the old bell signal a customer's entrance. Allen looked up to see a blonde-headed man enter the shop. He was dressed as any civilian would be, in a tan barn jacket and blue jeans; however, his body language was anything but that of a civilian. Allen closed the gift and stood at full alacrity without changing his body's expression at all.

"May I help you?" Allen offered with what was seemingly the portrait of casualness.

"Yes, I'm looking for a book on Benedict Arnold," a cold, raspy voice responded. "I'm fascinated with the psychology of traitors. Why would someone ever betray his own country? I can't understand it."

"Perhaps you have a faulty understanding of the word," Allen responded with ice in his blood, but warmth in his voice.

"There is no gray area for betrayal," the man retorted as he roamed about the store without meeting his green eyes to Allen's. "You either are a traitor, or you're not."

"Moral convictions play no part?" Allen examined while still maintaining an air of indifference.

"No," the blonde rebutted.

The stranger found what he was apparently looking for and approached the store worker, this time locking his hateful eyes with Allen's for the entire jaunt.

"You didn't truly think that if you stayed in one place, we wouldn't find you?" he asked. "Why be so stupid?"

"This is my home now."

"I'm not a particularly romantic man, but I'm sure you long ago surmised the irony of calling a place named after Purgatory your home," the stranger arrogantly stated.

"As I see it, my very existence is now a case for irony," Allen informed.

"Well, you weren't trained for things such as romance, nor was I," the stranger answered. "You were trained to obey rank and orders."

"I was given an order that was unthinkable," Allen enlightened.

"An order's an order," the blonde replied matter-of-factly.

"I couldn't follow orders that contradicted what I was and what I stood for. If they had such intentions for me, they never should have made me what they did," Allen lectured with his lips drawn tightly.

"If you had done what you were supposed to do eight weeks ago, the war would now be over," the man expounded in return.

"MAP had other agents for that. There are specific agents for that."

"They were on assignment elsewhere," the man dismissed.

"Doubtlessly," Allen sarcastically replied. "They realized I was becoming a Colossal; I was no longer simply a meta-agent. I was growing out of them. They gave me that order to remind me where I came from, and, in their eyes, what I was…"

"And now look at you," the man snarled with a sneer. "You're neither the Colossal that the people so desperately wanted you to be, nor are you a meta-agent. You're just a rogue, a runner, a traitor, a villain."

"You're from MAP, obviously, but who are you?" Allen scowled while fighting desperately to control his anger.

"I'm Agent 0104. I'm your replacement. My handle's going to be 'Anthem.' Can't say I'm going to enjoy having to act the clown that you did, but I am going to enjoy the completion of my first mission."

"What's that?" Allen growled without a hint of nervousness, although he knew his end was near.

"The location and termination of Agent 0099, code name: Freedom," Agent 0104 hissed. "In other words, killing our nation's greatest traitor."

"I'm no traitor…"

"I've been gathering intelligence for the last thirty-two hours, traitor. As soon as Agent Cyber-Spy got a bead on your position, they sent me to verify. Imagine my surprise to see a member of MAP serving coffee and flirting with a widow."

"I wasn't flirting," Allen bellowed.

"Calm yourself, traitor," Agent 0104 demanded. "You are currently within the crosshairs of Agent Shootdown. Make any sudden moves before I give the order for your termination, and Agent Shootdown will take matters into his own hands."

Agent 0104 was most pleased to see Allen turn his head slowly and look out the great window he stood alongside. Agent 0104 followed Allen's eyes until he was sure he saw the barrel of Shootdown's rifle on the rooftop across the street.

"It's not easy to kill members of MAP, traitor. My superiors know this, of course. That's why they designed a special caliber just for you. It'll pierce even our hides, if you believe any small arms fire can do such a thing. A shot to the temple—a guaranteed kill."

It was with glee that Agent 0104 finally saw a sign of nerves from Allen—a hard swallow—before Allen turned his blue stare back to the outsider.

"You know, the widow, Julie, I picked her name up easily in her shop while engaged in reconnaissance, she wouldn't be a widow right now if you had followed orders."

"Shut up," Allen commanded.

"The war would have been two weeks over around the time he was killed. Indeed, he may have even been coming home within the year. But you had to believe what the people of this great nation were saying about you. You believed you were the greatest of the Colossals. You ceased to be a soldier. Do you know how many men have died in Ulrakistan since you mutinied? Do you know how many men's deaths you are responsible for now?"

"Don't you think I feel that weight on my soul, on my conscience, Agent? Don't you think I've thought of nothing else since then?" Allen reacted with his cheeks grown flush in fury.

"Don't talk to me of souls and conscience, traitor. We don't have them. The fact that you look that woman next door in the eye is proof enough of that."

Allen calmed himself, and he then let out a long, deep sigh. Finally, he said, "Get this over with."

Agent 0104 pulled his collar up to his mouth and murmured something quietly. Allen quickly seized the gift left from Walter and held it to his chest, right against the heart he knew he had.

The sound was deafening.

***

Franklin and Julie bolted from Carmah's Cup after the rapport of the shot. They were horrified as they instantly saw the hole in Franklin's window that had taken out the "V" in Trover's Fine Literature.

"That's impossible," Julie heard Franklin mumble as he nearly paused to gape at the bullet hole.

The old man and young woman raced into Franklin's shop to find it completely empty.

"I'll check on Sophie," Julie screamed as she started to run to the back of the shop for the stairs leading to the apartment above.

"She took a ferry into Boston," Franklin muttered as his heart dropped.

Julie was momentarily relieved...until she saw what had caught Franklin's attention.

A trail of blood was peeking from around the corner of the front register counter. Both of them approached the counter slowly, and then they leaned over it.

Allen Hemmingway lay upon the floor with the Holy Bible held to his chest and a bullet hole upon his left temple.

***

"ETA in seven minutes, sir. You have orders over stealth comm. to suit up and await further orders..."

Agent 0099 grimaced at the soldier relaying orders to him. He released his straps and took his black satchel down from the overhead. He'd made quicker changes into uniform than this, seven minutes was an eternity. The agent unzipped the black satchel and pulled out the red, white, and blue uniform that his home country loved and trusted.

He'd had a bad feeling about this mission since he was called in twelve hours ago. After a debriefing that told him nothing other than the fact that he'd be going overseas and then given orders at the location, he geared up and moved out.

Now he found himself in what could only be black ops. The fact that he was to execute orders in uniform did not bode well. Agent 0099 loved his status as his nation's favorite Colossal. Unlike the other agents of MAP, he actually considered himself a Colossal and cared more about the purpose he served than the orders he was given. Thus far, the Superiors had used him only for moral boosting within home borders. He'd handled all Mega-Mals that crawled out of the garbage, and lives were saved. If that brought the people of his great nation closer to their government, well, that was an enormous perk. But, he contemplated long ago about what would happen if he was given an order that compromised his status as a Colossal. He had been frightened to think what he may do.

Today, his worst fear was about to come true.

Agent 0099 had just finished fastening on his G-Repulser when the solider began to speak:

"Your orders have just come through, sir."

"Proceed," Agent 0099 ordered.

Although the soldier had on a black visor and all Agent 0099 could see on it were the reflections of the surrounding red light within the tiny compartment of the plane, he somehow knew those eyes were wide in disbelief.

"Sir, you are to jettison in sixty seconds and reach these coordinates," the solider said as he handed Agent 0099 a gunmetal colored device lit up with green numbers.

The solider could not meet the ice-blue gaze that met his countenance after the agent looked back up from the coordinates.

"These coordinates…What are my orders?" the agent asked with glaciers stuck in his throat.

"Sir, after reaching the coordinates, you are to infiltrate the facility, then terminate target." With the completion of his last statement, the soldier reached to Agent 0099's device and pushed a button. The green numbers disappeared instantly and a picture of a man appeared.

Agent 0099's heart sank as he saw the image before his cold stare.

The day had finally come.

He knew exactly what the Superiors were up to. They knew he was the only member of MAP that fully welcomed being called a Colossal. They also knew that he was outgrowing them. He was expanding beyond their control. He was serving the people now, not the program. Apparently they felt it was time to reel Agent 0099 back in. They knew he'd never killed anyone during his years of service. They knew he valued his reputation as a heroic Colossal. It would be all over the international news in hours that Freedom had become nothing more than a common assassin. He was going to be just like all the other members of MAP. Agent Shootdown, Agent Hell Hound, Agent Cyber Spy, and all the rest had been given orders such as this in the past. Some didn't like it, some loved it, but they all had followed orders. Did he dare not?

"Soldier, you're positive orders were relayed correctly?" Agent 0099 sternly questioned.

"Yes, sir," the soldier answered. It was apparent that he did not disagree with the orders, only the choice of executioner. He tried to help with, "Agent 0099…Freedom," this caused Agent Freedom's head to snap to, "I know that you're a hero to the people of America. Hell, you're my hero, for cripe's sake! You're everyone's hero! But, you've got to think of the consequences of your actions. You plug this monster, and the war will be over. Ultimately, lives will be saved, sir."

"Where are the other agents, soldier?" Agent Freedom queried with bitterness.

He saw the soldier's head sink and that was all the answer he needed.

The Superiors were sending Freedom a message. In their eyes, he was just a lap dog. But, was that all he was? Was he just another soldier, beholden to any and all orders? Or was he also something else? The world had looked up to him over the last few years, virtually since his unveiling. Would the world ever forgive him for this act of hypocrisy?

"Ten seconds, sir," the soldier alerted.

Agent Freedom grabbed his now empty black satchel and approached the door of the jet. The soldier counted down and on "mark" rolled the door open. A whoosh of wind ripped through the vessel. Agent Freedom saw the soldier mouth good luck to him while counting down again with his fingers. When the last finger dropped, Agent Freedom flung himself into the star-filled night sky.

***

Crossing deserts.
Hiding in cargo trucks.
Stowing away in ships crossing oceans.
Swimming the final few miles to shore.
Why?
Why must he reach Purgatory Station?
Living on the streets.
Where was it?
Why was it so important that he get there?
What was the meaning behind Trover's Fine Literature?

***

Slowly the tiny blue slits opened almost completely. It was the first time they had done so in days. He saw a female figure hovering above him.

"Julie?" he mumbled.

He was greeted by a laugh that immediately told him that, no, this was not Julie. The voice was just as sweet, but far too aged. It could only be—

"Sophie…" he whispered with a smile.

"That's right, Allen," Sophie crooned while petting the hair back from his face, careful not to disturb the clean bandages she had just applied.

Allen reached up with a trembling, fatigued hand and felt the bandages upon his left temple. It's not the first time he'd ever been wounded severely, and he could tell simply by feeling the doctoring job that it'd been done well.

"Who dressed my wound?" Allen stammered in a weak voice while struggling to keep his eyes open and locked upon Sophie's.

"I did," Sophie answered. The attractive, elderly lady could see the surprise in the eyes of her patient and quickly informed, "I'm more than just Franklin's live-in gal pal, you know. Before I retired, I was an emergency room nurse. You don't honestly believe that this is the first gunshot wound I've treated during a lifetime of working in Purgatory Station, do you?"

"You're very good, ma'am, at field dressings."

Here was Sophie's sure sign that Allen was going to be fine. When he first gained consciousness, many things troubled her. She was troubled by his shaking hands, his weak voice, his drooping eyes; however, most of all, she was troubled by the fact that he called her simply "Sophie." She'd been either ma'am or Miss Sophie since Franklin had brought the young man up for some meatloaf several days ago. After hearing herself referred to once again as "ma'am," she was quite certain the boy was going to be just fine.

"Well, I think you're going to recover completely, as long as you give yourself a few weeks to heal."

"I should be fine in a few days," Allen said out loud without thinking. Sophie saw his eyes shoot up to her in alarm as he realized his mistake.

"Don't fret, child," she cooed. "I figured that your sort would heal up quite a bit quicker than a normal person. I won't tell your secret to anyone, don't worry."

"Ma'am?" Allen rejoined in complete guilelessness.

Sophie let out a long, chirp of a laugh and then voiced, "Oh, now, don't play that with me. Frankie doesn't remember that night, but I've been waiting for you since Wally spilled the beans all those years ago."

Allen quickly sprang up in his bed, causing himself the mother of all head rushes in the process, and looked at Sophie with an expression that words can't describe.

"Oh, I've got your attention now, do I?" she teased. "Well, I suppose I've just spilled the beans in a way myself, so I better get it out before that wound re-opens with your eyes as wide as they are.

"Oh, how to begin? Frankie told me that he shared with you how Wally came to live with us all those years ago—"

"*Wally*, ma'am?" Allen responded in perplexity.

Again, a big flash of white dentures, a laugh, and then Sophie sprang forth, "Those two are so formal with their 'Walter' and 'Franklin.' They'll always be 'Wally' and 'Frankie' to me. You're lucky I'm not calling you 'Alley.'" Once again, Sophie stopped to let out a bright giggle and even Allen smiled before she continued.

"Frankie hadn't been with us but a few weeks when those two yahoos got drunk off their buns for one of only a handful of times. I forget what the occasion was, I think they had convinced some big shot author to agree to a date for a signing in the shop. I can't remember.

"Anyway, the two boys were quite incapacitated, so I decided it was time for both to go to bed. Frankie needed more help than Wally, so, of course, big brother had to help me put his little brother in for the night. By the time we'd taken care of Frankie, the juice had caught up with Wally. He was a huge man, about your size, in fact, but even he couldn't drink all the whisky those fellas had gulped and not feel it eventually, so I found myself tucking Wally in also.

"Once I finally got him all tucked in, he was chatting like a drunk parrot. He started talking all about his job with the government."

Allen had been as stiff as a board while listening to Sophie recount the past, but now he grew even more rigid as he guessed his connection to this "Walter" was finally about to be revealed.

Sophie could see the anticipation in the young man's visage and tried to continue 'spilling the beans' as quickly as she could, "Walter was talking about how he used to be a bio-engineer/psychologist or some such with the government. Said that he'd been recruited to help with a soldier development program of sorts. It'd been going on since the forties, he told me, but they needed new scientists to carry on the program. What did he call that program?"

Sophie paused to ponder over her thoughts. Allen could see her searching the databanks of her brain and thought it rude to interrupt, although it took every effort on his part not to do so.

"MAT? No," Sophie corrected. "NAP? That's not right, either…"

"MAP," Allen finally informed as he at last saw the old gray eyes plead with him to help her remember.

"MAP! That's right! Mega-Agent Program, as I remember."

Allen chuckled, "Meta-Agent Program, actually." He knew he could be court-martialed for revealing such classified information, but since the government had already attempted an assassination upon him for, as they say, treason, he didn't see what the harm was at this point. How had he survived that gunshot, anyway? Agent 0104 had guaranteed him that the bullet being used would kill even a member of MAP, so how—? In due time, he hoped, he would find that answer out as well.

"Meta-Agent Program, that's right," the elderly lady grinned. Anyway, he was talking about how he had done the work of the devil. He was getting very emotional about it, and I could tell that he was greatly troubled by whatever he had been doing for them. I guess that's why he got out of it after he'd been attacked by some sort of dog."

Hell Hound sprung into Allen's mind instantly. It had to be Hell Hound. Allen had heard that Hell Hound had maimed several scientists during his development. It couldn't simply be a coincidence.

"He didn't agree with the work he was doing from a moral standpoint?" Allen inquired.

"That's right, he didn't agree with it at all," Sophie answered. "He said he was rearing the killers of tomorrow. He said it would all be in the name of truth, justice, and the American way, but they were still nothing more than killers."

"So he felt damned," Allen muttered.

"Not exactly," Sophie corrected. "In the midst of his tears, and that was the only time I'd ever seen Wally cry, by the way—I'm still waiting to see Frankie shed some of the waterworks—anyway, in the midst of his tears, he said that no matter how many killers he'd helped to develop, he had made a champion as well."

"A champion?" Allen choked out with a glimmer of hope struggling to be released.

"Yes, a champion," Sophie reaffirmed. She could see the longing in Allen's face and hoped that this would give him the peace that he so wanted. "Wally talked about the men and women he'd helped create who had no conscience and felt no guilt. They were bred to follow orders no matter what they thought of them. But there was one, he said, who, even as a child, had something he was not supposed to have."

Sophie watched as Allen began to lean forward.

"He said that there was a little boy, not even five years old, who he already knew from his evaluations could never be a killer. The boy had rejected all the psycho-tinkering that the lab rats had done to him. Wally said the boy would have been perfect in every way but one, according to his bosses—he had a con-science. But Wally made sure that the bosses would never find out about the boy's imperfection until it was too late. He said he was damned if he didn't let the boy develop, and he was damned if he did. He chose what his heart demanded, and he lied on the boy's evaluations."

The gray haired woman could see the workings of Allen's mind go into overdrive. She knew the boy already had deduced what she was going to tell him, after all, being above average intelligence probably *was* a component of being perfect.

"Wally finally began to drift off to sleep that night, Allen. Before he fell totally asleep, though, I asked him what he did about this boy with a con-science. He told me that he lied on his reports and allowed the boy to continue his training. He even recommended that the boy become the first of the Public Figure Program that MAP was thinking about. With all the Colossals springing up, apparently they thought they needed one of their own out there in the open.

"He told me that he knew it would only be a matter of time until the boy was given an order that he couldn't follow, so he placed a post-hypnotic sug-gestion in the boy that he was to immediately seek a specific location if he ever found himself on the outs with the government."

Allen began to shake. "What was the location?"

Sophie reached her hand out to Allen and lightly touched the young man on his cheek. She tested the bandage on his left temple, and after finding it to her satisfaction whispered, "The location was Trover's Fine Literature."

***

Later that evening, Allen was roused to see Franklin leaning over him with that old mustache of his partially framing a ripened smile.

"Good to see you, sir," Allen mumbled with a grin.

"Good to see you, too, son," Franklin returned while patting the injured man on the shoulder. "I thought we'd lost you when I saw all that blood."

"The temple area tends to bleed profusely," Allen informed while gently touching the bandage next to his left eye. "But I shouldn't have survived."

Franklin's slender eyebrows rose upon hearing Allen's rather matter-of-fact comment and exclaimed, "Preposterous! That bullet never should have hit you in the first place!"

Allen could only presume that this was some insinuation that the aged storeowner wanted an explanation as to why his front window now had a large hole in it. However, Allen had some things he needed to know first, such as, how was he able to survive a bullet that had been designed specifically for killing MAP members.

"Sir," the wounded man began, despite noticing Franklin's agitation at being called "sir" incessantly. "I realize that you need to know why I was shot—"

Allen stopped a moment as he saw Franklin begin to protest, but something in his sometimes cold blue eyes communicated that he wished to finish, "—but there are some things that I need to know first. Describe the exact circumstances of my being found. I can only assume it was you who brought me up here."

"Well," Franklin began uncomfortably, "I'm afraid that I couldn't lift you alone, you're an awfully big boy. I had to have Julie help me—"

"What!" Allen cried out in astonishment.

"Not to worry, Allen," Franklin consoled. "I told her that you were simply grazed by the bullet."

Franklin could see the multitude of thoughts flashing through the dark headed man's eyes and quickly reported, "When we came into the store, she started to run upstairs to find Sophie, but I told her that Sophie had gone to Boston. I said this as I leaned over the counter to find the source of all that blood. That's when I saw you laying on the floor with the Bible held to your chest."

Allen quickly looked to his nightstand and saw his most cherished possession, left to him by Walter, awaiting his next visit. It now had some rust-colored stains upon it.

Franklin continued, "Julie immediately began to scream and put her hands over her eyes. She started to stumble back, so I'm relatively sure she didn't see what I saw. I saw *this* sticking three-quarters out of your left temple." Franklin reached into his pants' pocket and pulled out one of the biggest bullets either man had ever seen in their lives. "I've got no idea what caliber this monster is…"

"There is no name for its caliber. That bullet doesn't even officially exist," Allen hissed out. He wasn't angry with Franklin. He was angry with himself. Although he knew he was the target of this Agent 0104, or "Anthem" as the mystery man called himself, it is doubtless that if anyone else had been in the shop that they would have been terminated as well. One thing about MAP, if it didn't want to be seen, it wouldn't.

"Yeah, you're probably right. That's why I went ahead and handled it," the clever old man admitted. "I figured we wouldn't be able to trace it anyway, so my fingerprints wouldn't hurt it any."

"Sir," Allen tested with hesitation in his voice. "Aren't you curious as to why that bullet didn't kill me? You seem to be awfully calm about this."

"Actually, young man, I was just thinking the same thing about you!" Franklin let out with a huff.

Allen Hemmingway's eyes grew large at this statement and he had no idea how to reply. What was that supposed to mean?

Franklin smirked and continued, "I slid the bloody bullet into my pocket and yelled at Julie to call Sophie. I knew that she'd be able to patch that wound up. If it'd gone any deeper, I don't know what I'd have done."

"Not that I'm complaining, sir, but why didn't you take me to a hospital?" Allen inquired.

Franklin laughed and said, "Julie argued that same point. She demanded we call 911, not Sophie. I've never had any children, Allen, not of my own, but I used the best parent voice I had, and I told Julie to go call Sophie and trust me. Well, that got her moving. I didn't mention the fact to her that a man who uses a fake name would not like to find himself in a public hospital. Am I right?"

"Does she realize it's fake also?"

"Julie's a smart young woman, Allen. Smart enough to know when not to ask a man why he's covering up his real identity. But I like to think that she knows the good guys from the bad guys. I figure that's why she doesn't badger us about who you really are."

Allen winced at this. He thought of Trent, Julie's husband that had died weeks after he had defied orders. Trent, who in all likelihood, would still be alive today if Allen had done what he was told. Trent—a man who left a widow and a kid brother. Trent—a man who Allen found himself becoming jealous of whenever he thought of Julie.

"I tried to haul you upstairs while she called Sophie to come back, but you're too darn heavy! I had to wait for her to get back and it took us twenty minutes to get you up the steps. We finally got you up here, though, and did the best we could with stopping the bleeding. I was worried you were going to hemorrhage to death before Sophie got back. But, she finally arrived after taking a cab all the way from Boston. She stitched you up just in time, according to her. She does tend to have a knack for the dramatic, however, so who's to say for sure..."

Although he already knew the answer due to the fact that Franklin and Julie were still breathing, Allen asked anyway, "So no one was in the store or the apartment after you and Julie arrived?"

"Well," Franklin's voice began to tremble while he rubbed the back of his head and sat on the side of Allen's bed. "No. No one was here. But your room was a disaster, as though someone had sifted though all of your things. Your window was open as well. I think whoever it was, we just missed him..."

"Thank God," Allen whispered to himself. "Was anything missing?"

Franklin could hear the concern in Allen's voice and said, "No, son. Everything seemed to still be here, just out of place. Of course, I didn't see that black satchel of yours, but I haven't seen *it* in quite a while."

"It's fine," Allen interjected harshly, and instantly regretted his tone. He couldn't hide the rage he was feeling with himself for putting his friends at risk. It's obvious what Agent 0104 was looking for. He didn't just have orders to terminate Agent Freedom; he had orders to retrieve some very expensive equipment as well. A belt that allows a man to fly is not something that the government merely writes off.

"I'm glad you're all safe," he said with his eyes down and his hand on Franklin's shoulder.

"We're glad you're safe as well, young fella," Franklin returned with the most kindness that Allen had ever heard. "Julie's going to come see you later. She's beside herself she's so happy that you're going to be well. She's a beautiful young woman, isn't she?" the old man hinted.

Allen grew sick to his stomach with self-loathing and wished to change the subject, "So, you seem to have a theory as to how I survived. May I hear it?"

The shopkeeper began to shake his head back and forth in puzzlement and pondered, "You never should have been hit in the first place!"

"Why?"

"Until you walked into my shop I never had a clue as to why, but years ago Walter insisted that we install the highest quality bulletproof glass available.

And when I say available, I don't mean on the open market. He knew some people from his old government job that owed him a favor, as he put it.

"I guess that there must have been a weak point where the bullet hit. That's all that I can figure. Otherwise, a bullet fired from a handgun or rifle, no matter how big it is, should never have breached the glass."

Allen knew better, however. MAP agents were built tough, and their skin was more resistant than any known bulletproof glass. It was only the combination of the two that saved his life. Once again, Walter, a man he had no recollection of knowing, had proven his savior.

***

He knew she had entered before he had even opened his eyes. It was her perfume; it lit his heart on fire every time he smelled it.

"Hi, Julie," he greeted as he opened his eyes and sat up.

Allen couldn't help but notice that Julie appeared as though she was going on a date later. Her curly hair was done beautifully and hung loosely about her shoulders. She wore a lovely black shirt with a khaki skirt. Allen even noted that her fingernails had been freshly painted. He hated himself for it, but his heart grew envious of whomever it was she had a date with.

"Hi, big guy," she offered playfully. She sat on the edge of his bed, and he tried very hard not to notice her arm brushing his leg as she propped herself to one side. "How are you feeling?"

"I'm feeling better." Indeed, Allen was feeling much better. It had been nearly twenty-four hours since his injury. He had been engineered to heal quickly. He didn't feel it was necessary to share that information, of course. Any nagging pain had hurriedly disappeared at the sight of the gorgeous brunette.

"We'll need to get you a new one," Julie whispered as she pointed to Allen's stained Bible on the nightstand.

"No, that one was left to me for a reason. I'll never replace it," Allen returned.

Julie simply nodded her head in understanding. She then reached out and touched the bandage on his left temple. After inspecting it to her liking, she took her hand away and rubbed his cheek gently as she did so. Allen loved it and hated himself for loving it.

"Do you have a date later?" Allen asked, trying to district himself from the pleasure of her touch.

"No, why?" she answered.

Allen found himself speechless.

Julie, however, did not, "Allen, I'm sorry, but I'm not like Franklin. I have to know. Why were you shot? Why do you use a fake name? You're obviously in some kind of trouble. I need to know what's going on."

Julie saw Allen's jaw begin to clench tightly. His blue eyes stared deeply into her soul. She perceived his mind racing. She knew this was a lost cause. He wasn't going to tell her.

"I know that I have no right to ask you anything. We just met, after all—"

"Julie—" Allen tried to interrupt.

"—but I always assumed I'd never find anyone else after Trent. I never wanted anyone else. Trent was my hero. I loved him more than life, but now he's gone. I feel like I haven't grieved long enough, but—"

"—please don't do this," Allen moaned.

Julie continued anyway, "Allen, I don't even know your real name, but I'm feeling something for you that I haven't felt for anyone but Trent. I can't lose someone else that I feel this way about. I don't know why I have these feelings for a man who won't even tell me his real name, but I do. Please Allen, tell me what's going on. Who are you?"

Allen let out a deep groan. He knew this moment would come. Ever since he saw Julie and then learned of her husband and his death, he knew this moment would come. The confession. The problem is that he never dreamt that she would have feelings for him. However, she just admitted as much. He could hang up his uniform forever. As far as the Superiors were concerned, Freedom was dead. Agent 0099 was targeted by Anthem and terminated by Shootdown. As long as the G-Respulser never resurfaced, he could live a life with Julie. Freedom was dead. He could stay that way. Allen Hemmingway could live on.

No. He owes Trent the truth. Although he never met Trent, he owes him that much. Like all those others, Trent died defending the nation. Allen couldn't take his life and then his wife as well. The truth must be told. Freedom is a Colossal, and Colossals must do the right thing.

"Julie," Allen began with hesitation. "There's something I have to tell you." His eyes locked with Julie's and he whispered out of fear, "I'm a fugitive of the government. I was ordered to kill someone eight weeks ago, and I defied orders."

Julie's eyes grew huge. "Who were you supposed to kill?"

Even though he wanted to drop his eyes from hers, he wouldn't let himself. "If I had killed this person, the war in Ulrakistan would, in all likelihood, be over right now. I'm certain it would have ended two months ago.

"I was shot because I'm considered a traitor by the government. They think I'm dead, and as long as I keep a low profile, they won't bother me again.

"I'm not a killer, Julie. I never have been. I couldn't follow that order, even though it meant—"

"Trent would still be alive..." Julie mumbled as she tore her gaze from Allen's.

"Not just Trent, Julie. Hundreds more would still be alive. It was the hardest decision of my life, but I couldn't carry out that order—"

"WHY?" Julie screamed at Allen while bursting to her feet. "What makes you so high and mighty that you can defy orders? Trent had to follow orders all the time that he hated, because that's what a good soldier does! That's what loyal soldiers do! They follow orders to keep other soldiers alive!"

"I was more than just a soldier, Julie..."

Julie's mouth set rigid as tears began to roll down her red cheeks. They left black trails behind them. "No, you weren't more than a soldier. Because if you were, that means that you were better than Trent, and you're not half the man that Trent was. I can't believe that I almost tainted his memory by thinking you were even close to being what he was to me..."

Allen tried to stand from his bed, but immediately became lightheaded from the sudden movement. "Julie," he started as he fell back down onto the bed, "please, don't go. I can't make it up to you, but try to understand—"

"NO!" Julie turned in his doorway and burned hatred through him with her eyes. "You understand this—You ARE a traitor! Whether you're a traitor or not to the government, I'll let God decide. But I know you're a traitor to Trent, and a traitor to me! If I ever see you step foot in my shop again, I *will* call the FBI, or CIA, or whoever it takes! I'll turn you in, whoever you are, so stay away! Don't ever talk to me or look at me again!"

Allen's wound may have been healing, but after seeing Julie storm from his room, he had a new injury that he was sure would never heal. All the engineering in the world couldn't help him now.

***

"It's been days..." Allen muttered.

"I know, Allen, but things take time. You sure you don't want to tell me exactly what happened?" Sophie responded as she handed him his coffee from across the breakfast bar.

Allen reached out and felt the warmth against the palm of his hand. It was the only warmth he'd felt since Julie had left his life forever. He was sitting on a stool with his back to the living room and faced Sophie while she was preparing lunch in the kitchen.

"I'm sorry, ma—er, Miss Sophie, but saying what I had to tell Julie was hard enough. I'd prefer not to get into it again. I had to say it to her; it was a matter of duty."

"You always do your duty, don't you?" Sophie stated rather matter-of-factly as she dropped noodles into boiling water.

"No, I don't," Allen seethed with self-hatred.

Sophie turned around from the stove and reached her hand out to Allen's. She felt the heat left over from the coffee cup on his skin and confirmed, "You do follow your duty, Allen. You may not follow the duties given to you by some, but you follow the duty given to you by your most important superior." At the conclusion of this statement, Sophie purposefully gazed at something.

Allen followed her gaze and saw it resting on his Bible that was comfortably next to him on the counter. It was open to the place he had last left off reading.

"What are you saying?" Allen prodded.

"I'm saying that sometimes you have to follow your heart. If you're meant to be something, and you succeed at that something, your heart will be at ease. If you're meant to be something else, your heart will pine until you are that something else. One thing may not be more right or wrong than the other may. You are what you are, Allen, and you can't be anything else. Whether Julie agrees with what you are or not, you must remain true to your calling."

"I no longer heed my calling," Allen said below his breath.

"I hope that's not true," Franklin's voice interrupted from behind.

Allen and Sophie turned to see Franklin climbing the steps from the shop below. He quickly ran to the television set and demanded that Allen and Sophie come see what's on.

"Who's tending the store?" Sophie asked.

"Store's closed!" Franklin exclaimed.

"Why?" Allen inquired.

"Because the Mayor's ordered all of Old Downtown to close up and take cover!"

Franklin found the channel he wanted and pointed to the set. Sophie and Allen peered at the screen and saw a huge, human-shaped rock trudging along, tossing cars and busses and anything else that got in its way to the side.

"What is that?" Allen spouted with grave concern.

"That, young man, is what Purgatory Station dubbed 'The Nether Man' long before you or I were born," Franklin answered very seriously.

"What is it?" Sophie questioned.

Franklin shrugged his shoulders and returned, "It's just what it looks like, a giant rock-man!"

"Is it hostile?" Allen interrogated with his eyes narrowed. He could feel the calling.

"Depends on your idea of 'hostile,' Allen." Franklin could see the perplexity in Allen's eyes so he gave a quick update, "This thing shows up every once in a while and wreaks havoc on the city. Last time Purgatory Station saw him was in 1901, so when I say every once in a while, I'm serious! He's never been stopped; he just surfaces out of the Atlantic, crosses our island, and then walks right back into the ocean! It's like he's some kind of a nomad."

"What's his purpose?"

"He doesn't appear to have one," Franklin said in reply to Allen's question. "You know I've been known to keep up with this city's Colossals and Mega-Mals—"

Sophie interjected with a huffy, "That's an understatement!"

Franklin, having chosen to apparently ignore her, continued on, "This fella first showed up in the late seventeen hundreds, back when this city was just a house of detention for what the Puritans felt were the worst of irredeemable sinners. He's never been seen anywhere else but here. Legend has it that he was a fella that killed himself on the north side of the island in what's now Wilderness Park next to the Historic District. Problem is, he supposedly committed suicide on a cursed rock. According to the myth, his soul became trapped within the rock and he's been stuck inside of it ever since, doomed to wander the island and the surrounding ocean floors for all eternity."

"You're serious?" Allen asked incredulously with an eyebrow raised.

"I'm as serious as bulletproof skin," Franklin responded with a smirk.

"Can it be stopped?"

"Never has in the past—"

Franklin stopped talking as he noticed Allen's attention distracted by the newscast on the television. On the screen the reporter was talking about a new Colossal dubbed "Anthem" that showed up on the scene a few minutes ago to challenge the Nether Man.

Allen saw the black-suited agent with a big red "A" on his chest and a blue cape try to punch the Nether Man. It wasn't quite without satisfaction when he saw Anthem go flying into a building after the Nether Man responded to Anthem's blow with a very solid roundhouse.

Anthem next tried bullets against the rock-man with his forearm mounted semi-automatic weapon. That was to no avail as well, and for Anthem's efforts the Nether Man tossed a bus in his direction.

Allen wondered how long it would take Anthem to regain consciousness.

"Fella's going about it the wrong way," Franklin mumbled.

"What do you mean?" Allen asked.

"The Nether Man can't be stopped. You just have to get out of his way and hope his tour of the city isn't going to be a long one. There's no record of it being a murderer outright, to kill simply for the sake of killing, but it has killed before. Lots of folks in the past have been killed simply because they were in the way. That Colossal should be trying to get people away, not taking it on man-to-man."

"He's no Colossal," Allen grunted with his lips in a snarl.

"Well, if that's the case, I think we could use a Colossal who respects life on the scene," Sophie uttered directly to Allen.

"I think Allen could use some rest, don't you?" Franklin asked his live-in lady-friend.

"Yes, I think so. Allen, why don't you go take a nap and rest that head up of yours. We won't wake you up for a few hours, so don't worry about us coming into your room. Be sure to take the bandage off before you get into bed, though."

Allen smiled at the old couple as he got up from the couch.

"You're sure there's no way that thing can be stopped?"

"Allen, I've told you everything I know about it. How do you stop a soul encased within a cursed rock? I have no idea. I just hope whoever helps this Anthem fella can get the people out of its way!"

A soul within a cursed rock. Allen could relate.

***

He entered his bedroom and slid the bed off to the side. Once the bed was out of the way, he removed the loose floorboards and took out his black satchel. After unzipping it, he pulled out the red, white, and blue uniform. He then pulled out his gauntlets, followed by his boots, and finally, the G-Respulser.

They'll kill him to get it back.

But not before he saved some lives.

***

The skylight on top of Franklin Trover's building was thrust open and Freedom burst through it towards the mayhem of the Nether Man.

* * *

The bus was on top of him in such a way that he could get no leverage to lift it. Any other members of MAP may have had concerns that they'd be able to lift it in the first place, but Anthem, or Agent 0104, never had any problems in the "I can" department. Even so, he was going to need some sort of a foothold if he was going to budge it.

"Damn it," he muttered to himself. "First time out in this clown suit, and I've been buried alive by a bus thrown by a rock-man. Black Ops is where I belong, not this garbage."

He gave one last push with all his might, and the bus amazingly lifted from his chest. It was quickly tipped to the right, and Anthem found himself staring up at a big red "F."

"You're dead," Anthem growled.

"I guess I've been resurrected," Freedom answered with an uncommon arrogance.

Anthem brushed the debris from him and stood up. He was only slightly taller than Freedom.

"I'll deal with you after the freak," Anthem assured as he turned and walked away from Freedom, the overturned bus, and the rest of the chaos that the Nether Man had left in his wake.

"You won't be able to stop him with sheer force," Freedom called out.

Freedom knew exactly what was happening when he saw Anthem stop in his tracks, glance back at him, and say, "I'll stop him. By any means necessary." The more experienced Colossal knew that this was a make or break mission for Anthem. He had to stop the Nether Man. Freedom realized that this was his official debut as far as the nation was concerned, and if Anthem was going to replace America's greatest Colossal, that being himself, then he couldn't afford to take a loss. This made Anthem very dangerous in Freedom's eyes. Anthem would win, no matter what the cost. Even if it took the deaths of a few civilians to guarantee his victory.

Freedom lifted off thanks to the G-Respulser and landed directly in front of Anthem. He stared into the star-shaped visor that gave him his own reflection in return and snarled, "I won't let any civilians be harmed in this mission, Agent 0104. Whatever you've got planned, you better clear it with me first."

Anthem roughly shoved his way past Freedom and hissed, "You hold no rank, traitor, so don't give me orders. But if you say that nothing can stop that thing, well, that leaves me no choice. I'm calling in an air strike."

Freedom's eyes grew huge while he quickly took an inventory of the human loss that was about to happen. There were camera crews and reporters everywhere, not to mention all of the people taking cover in the buildings along the surrounding blocks. Although this inventory took only seconds, when he returned his gaze to Anthem, he saw the vicious agent pulling his comm-link in closer. Without a moment's hesitation, Freedom shot out a red-gauntlet, turned Anthem around so that he faced Freedom, and then tore the comm-link loose from Anthem's headpiece. Any communication with whoever was giving and receiving instructions from Anthem was now terminated.

Anthem raised his weapon to Freedom's chest and stuck the barrel right to his heart.

"Look around you, Agent," Freedom muttered. "You're my replacement, yes, but you don't want the people to see you actually execute my needing replaced, do you?"

Anthem slowly turned his head and saw the camera crews filming his every move. "You're lucky, traitor…"

***

"It's so great to see him again!" Nick shouted with joy.

Julie, Nick, Sophie, and Franklin sat in the living room of Julie's apartment above her shop, Carmah's Cup. Franklin insisted that they take refuge together, whatever her feelings may be about Allen. Julie didn't even ask Franklin where Allen was, her hatred seemed to run that deep.

"This is Sydney Attwater with WPUG news, where the legendary Nether Man has finally returned, along with Freedom, the long-absent Colossal. We also have a new Colossal on the scene, but we have yet to learn his name. It would appear that this new Colossal and Freedom appear to be acquainted, but, judging from their body language, it is not a friendly acquaintance. Indeed, the blonde man in black went so far as to point his weapon against Freedom's chest," the reporter from the television accounted.

"I wonder what caliber the fella's got in his gun," Franklin whispered into Sophie's ear. Sophie gave him a very concerned look in return.

"Julie, isn't it great?" Nick yelled with glee to his sister-in-law. "I knew he'd be back! Just when Purgatory Station needed him most!"

Julie only let out a disgusted sigh as a response.

The news reporter continued, "Apparently having settled their differences, Freedom and the other Colossal have both lifted off and are heading south on Geoff Avenue to catch up with the Nether Man. The Mayor is urging all citizens in Old Downtown to seek refuge. Remember that it has been one hundred and three years since the Nether Man was last seen. There are many in this city that doubted its existence at all! Well, as this reporter can attest, the Nether Man is very real! This is Sydney Attwater—"

"South on Geoff Avenue, they're heading right for us!" Nick smiled widely. "Maybe we'll get to see them in person! I'm going down to the shop for a better look!"

"You're staying right here!" Julie commanded with stone in her voice.

"But, Julie, it could be my only chance to see a hero! Besides Trent, I've never seen a real hero!" Nick begged.

Julie mumbled, "You won't see a real one today, either."

Franklin and Sophie squeezed each other's hands, not sure how to take Julie's last comment.

***

Freedom and Anthem flew in low at thirty miles per hour. Anthem wanted to hit the Nether Man high from behind and have Freedom hit him low, but Freedom had to convince the other man that would do nothing but give them each a concussion. For some reason, Anthem refused to accept that the Nether Man was made of pure rock. Freedom supposed that it would be difficult for a man that hadn't been fighting Mega-Mals like the Black Hole or the Fog Master for years to accept that there existed enemies that were more than just flesh and blood wielding man-made weapons.

"What is your tactic, then, traitor? After all, if you hadn't destroyed my comm-link, this thing would now be a pile of debris."

"And so would most of Old Downtown, Anthem! Do you even think of the lives at stake?" Freedom argued.

"This coming from the man who is responsible for a war's continuance?" Anthem assaulted with an obnoxious smirk.

Freedom did not give a repartee.

Anthem and Freedom flew over the Nether Man's head and landed twenty meters ahead of it. They both turned and faced the monster and waited for his approach. Freedom could see that the creature was not angry, it was not in a rage. It simply walked. If an empty vehicle happened to be in its path, he tossed it aside with a shrug. That was the story with anything that got in its way, and

Freedom was there to make sure that nobody found themselves in the Nether Man's path. He looked around and saw no one on the street, and that was good. Unfortunately, he did note several faces pressed up against the windows of the surrounding buildings as though they were watching a sporting event. Should the Nether Man deviate from its course of following Geoff Avenue and begin infiltrating buildings, Freedom didn't dare think of the casualties.

"What this thing's story, traitor?" Anthem yelled over the explosion of a car's gas tank igniting. Freedom could not see if the other agent was shocked to observe the Nether Man emerge from the flames.

"Supposedly, it's a cursed rock with a man's soul trapped within."

Anthem turned his head and stared at Freedom.

"I'm serious," the dark haired man grumbled. "NO!"

Freedom saw another car get tossed out of the creature's path, but this one was heading straight for a diner with many patrons pressed to the windows. In an instant, Freedom lifted from the ground and sped to intercept the car. There was no way he could catch it with its momentum and no leverage of his own to be had, so he instead opted to ram it from the side and force it to land harmlessly on the sidewalk. The plan worked perfectly, except for the fact that when he thought 'harmlessly,' he failed to take into account the impact damage to his shoulder. By his count, though, no one had died…yet.

Freedom waved to the people in the diner with his remaining good arm and then turned to soar back to the Nether Man. As he neared it, he was disgusted to see Anthem pick up a motorcycle and throw it into the Nether Man. It did not even slow the creature's stride as it broke into a million pieces.

"Follow me!" Freedom cried as he swooped past Anthem. Anthem lifted off thanks to his own G-Respulser and followed in Freedom's slipstream. They finally landed and turned toward the creature that was now a quarter of a mile behind them. It was time to regroup and develop some semblance of strategy. Freedom had a long shot of an idea.

He did not notice that they were standing directly in front of Carmah's Cup.

"First Redeemer is two blocks west of here, Agent. Bring me back a priest!" Freedom ordered.

"What?" Anthem blurted out in confusion.

"We've got to stop this thing. The city's only getting more populated; if we let it run its path, it could return later and cause even more loss of life. Today we stop it."

"What does a priest have to do with that?" Anthem hatefully roared with cynicism.

Just then Freedom saw a fire truck speed into the Nether Man at the intersection of Geoff and O'Neil. He'd heard the sirens, but there were sirens going off everywhere from the damaged vehicles and buildings, the fires left in the creature's wake, and as a general warning to the civilians. The truck accidentally engulfed the creature, and Freedom's eyes nearly grew watery as he realized that the Nether Man had just claimed its first lives during this excursion.

"Get the priest!" Freedom barked and then hurled himself towards the truck.

Freedom did not see Anthem give him the finger before flying west in search of First Redeemer and the priest. Freedom only saw the men that were still alive trapped within the fire truck. The trick was going to be to dislodge the Nether Man before it began thrashing the truck from its body. Once it started pulling the truck from itself, the casualties on that truck would be even more horrendous.

Freedom banked right and then turned sharply left. He would ram the truck from its front and hopefully push it backwards, dislodging the monster stuck within its grill. He'd just have to be sure to lead with his left shoulder this time.

The impact was devastating to Freedom's other shoulder, but the truck was freed, the Nether Man was released, and lives were saved. Freedom could do nothing as the Nether Man continued his trek southbound until after he had checked on all the surviving firemen. After making sure they were relatively fine, he pulled back the mangled frame so that they could retrieve their fallen comrades. They quickly covered their brothers and then went to work on the surrounding fires. Duty called them to action, no matter what their emotions demanded. Freedom knew that they were the true Colossals of the world. He quickly bent to one knee and prayed over the fallen men, and then he followed his duty as well.

As Freedom approached the Nether Man again, he experienced fear in a form he had never dealt with before. How could he not have noticed his surroundings? The Nether Man was just meters away from Carmah's Cup and Trover's Fine Literature. That is not what put fear's icy scythe through his heart, however. The true fear came from seeing Nick popping out of the front door of Julie's coffee shop. The true fear came from seeing the Nether Man toss another car, this time in a direct course for the redheaded boy who was waving too frantically at Freedom to notice the yellow sports car jetting towards him. Freedom pushed the G-Respulser to its limits as it kicked into high gear, and he prayed he could go three for three.

He knew his shoulders couldn't take another shot, so he'd have to do this the old fashioned way. Could he catch a car standing flat-footed? He'd find out soon enough.

"Oh my gosh, Freedom, I can't believe it's yo—ahhhhh!"

Freedom was thankful to the CEO of the sky, as Franklin put it, for having Nick prop the door to Carmah's Cup open with his back as he waved like a madman. He was able to land, push the boy into the coffee shop as gently as he could, which in this case would surely result in bruised ribs for the redhead, and turn to face the impending car.

He didn't even have time to get his hands up.

The car hit him directly in the chest and pinned him against the doorframe of Julie's shop. To say that he was in pain could easily have been the biggest understatement since the last time the Nether Man had visited.

He heard the boy crying from inside the shop, but he knew the fifteen-year-old would be fine. He had no such sure feelings about his own outcome, however. Especially since the Nether Man was now finally and impossibly stopped dead in his tracks.

Anthem had dropped the priest right in front of the creature and then looked at Freedom for further instruction. Freedom could tell by Anthem's body language that it was killing him to take orders from Freedom, and he understood that this would be the last time that the other agent would ever take commands from him.

What surprised Freedom more than anything, however, was the priest! The priest actually had his fists raised expertly as though he was going to attempt to combat the Nether Man!

"No, Father! You're not here to fight it!" Freedom yelled from the wreck of the car around him.

"What the hell's he supposed to do, then?" Anthem shouted back as he was in the middle of reloading his gauntlet's gun.

"I'm a pastor!" the pastor hollered immediately after Anthem, and then followed with, "And you watch your language."

Freedom would have laughed if the situation was not so serious, and if he hadn't noticed his vision going black around the edges.

"Pastor, tell it to move on!"

The middle-aged man known to his congregation as Pastor Irons returned with, "What are you talking about?"

Freedom, fighting to stay conscious, clamored back, "It's got the soul of a man who killed himself stuck in it. Tell it to move on; tell it that its time in Purgatory is now over!"

A light seemed to go on in Pastor Irons' eyes. Anthem seemed more confused than ever.

Freedom watched with dimming eyesight as the pastor lifted his cross up into the air while the Nether Man lifted its great, stony arms high above the pastor's head. Anthem also lifted his left arm, as well, and prepared to let loose a volley of useless bullets.

And then Freedom went dark.

***

"You may address me as Anthem, and you'll be seeing me whenever a Mega-Mal such as this one appears."

"Anthem, are you and Freedom partners?" he heard Sydney Attwater ask.

Freedom slowly opened his eyes to see Anthem giving an interview to a reporter. He saw this over the top of the car that was still pinning him against the doorframe of Carmah's Cup. Anthem had him. He was trapped. They wouldn't have to terminate him in public now, they'd just show up, haul him away, and no one would ever see him again.

It was worth it, though. He couldn't handle another death of a Carmah on his soul.

Apparently his plan had worked. The Nether Man was in the exact same position it had been in when he had passed out. The eerie brimstone light that had been glowing from its eyes was now gone, and Freedom hoped that meant that the soul that was powering them was gone as well. Gone where, he couldn't say for sure. But gone, nonetheless.

Freedom closed his eyes and awaited *his* outcome.

"Negative. Freedom is no partner of mine," Anthem informed with rigid dislike in response to Sydney Attwater's most recent question. "In fact, there's something that you all should know about Freedom. This man is nothing more than—"

"A hero!" a new voice shouted out. "This man, Freedom, is a hero, and we should all thank him!"

He smelled her wonderful perfume before he even opened his eyes.

"This man saved my brother-in-law's life. The least we could do is free him from that car!"

Freedom perceived a vision of beauty crawling out from the huge broken window of Carmah's Cup. This was the same beauty that was doing her best to get him away from Anthem.

He heard a groan and saw that Pastor Irons had been pushing on the car all along, but to no avail. Still, he wondered why a middle-aged pastor would have biceps the size of his own bulging out of his shirt sleeves. Freedom took note.

He next saw Franklin, Sophie, and a bruised Nick crawl through the window as well. They all went to work on the car. Even Sidney Attwater stopped her interview of Anthem as she and her camera crew leant a hand.

"Don't I know you?" Freedom heard Franklin ask. He assumed it was directed towards him as an inside joke.

"I don't think so," he heard Pastor Irons return quickly.

"You could help, you know," Julie called out to Anthem.

Freedom watched in amusement as Anthem realized that while his interview with Sidney Attwater may be postponed; there were still plenty of cameras recording the situation. How could the nation's newest Colossal not help the nation's favorite Colossal?

Anthem steamed at the civilians to get out of the way, and then he tore the wreckage, rather barbarously, from Freedom's body.

Finally, Freedom could breathe again.

Sydney Attwater was immediately taking advantage of the situation. "So, Freedom and Anthem, seemingly a rather patriotic pair! I wonder if you might give me an exclusive interview about your battle against and final defeat of the Nether Man."

"Why don't you continue on with Anthem, he did all of the exasperating work. I just caught a few cars," Freedom said with a smile. "Besides, I think I need to say hello to a friend."

Freedom chuckled as he read a rather rude command from Agent Anthem's lips while Sydney continued her interview.

"How are you?" Freedom asked as he approached his friend.

"Oh, my gosh! It's you! It's really you!" Nick stammered.

Freedom beamed at the boy even though his insides were on fire. The boy seemed not to even register his own bruised ribs after Freedom had tossed him away from the door.

"Nick, try to calm down," Julie coldly ordered her brother-in-law.

Nick looked at her in confusion as she stood with Sophie and Franklin, and then questioned, "But Julie, he saved my life! If you can't get excited over your hero, who can you get excited over?"

"I'm not a hero, Nick," Freedom clarified. "I'm just a man who tries to do the right thing. Sometimes the consequences of my decisions are good, sometimes they aren't. But my conscience is my only compass, and I have to live by it."

Nick looked up at Freedom in obvious bewilderment. Julie, on the other hand, could not bring herself to meet the eyes of the Colossal known publicly as Freedom, nor could she return the gaze of the man known as Allen Hemmingway.

"But you are a hero, Freedom," Nick affirmed as he admired the towering man. "You're just like my brother, Trent. I want to be just like both of you someday!"

Freedom put his hand on Nick's shoulder and replied, "It's an honor for you to compare me to your brother, Nick. But trust me, he's the real hero. Remember that."

Freedom looked at Julie one last time and felt his heart drop as she refused to meet his pleading eyes. He then nodded to Franklin and Sophie who waved to him in return. He next looked at Nick one last time and said, "This country owes men and women like your brother for the sacrifices they make on a routine basis, Nick. Thanks to you and all the others who give us their family members so that we may live on in freedom."

A tear fell from Nick's eyes and he whispered something that only Freedom could hear.

Freedom turned away from those he considered his family and called out to Sidney Attwater, "We'll have to do it another time, Ms. Attwater. I've got to fly."

And with that, Freedom lifted off and disappeared high into the evening's glowing sky.

"This interview is over," Anthem snapped at Sydney as he started after Freedom.

"Nick," Julie began as she took note of Anthem's action, "why don't you go ask our newest Colossal for his autograph?"

"Great idea!" Nick replied as he ran off towards Anthem.

Julie, Sophie, and Franklin watched, bemused, as Nick and several other neighborhood children delayed Anthem's pursuit of the wounded Freedom. Sydney Attwater was even kind enough to give the children paper so that each and every one of them could get a coveted autograph from the nation's newest Colossal.

Anthem looked as though he could spit venom.

***

A few days later, Julie heard the buzz signal the arrival of a new customer and left her pastries to approach the front counter. Her heart sank as she saw the man walk through the construction workers that were rebuilding the front of her shop and stand before her.

"Thank you, Julie, for helping me out with Anthem the other day. You kept me from being taken in. I'll always remember that."

"I did it for Nick," Julie answered coldly. "I couldn't stand him losing you and Trent within the same year. I didn't do it for you. Just remember that."

Allen shifted uncomfortably, but he continued nevertheless, "What I said, about the nation owing you and Nick a debt of gratitude for giving up your loved one to us, I meant that."

Julie said nothing.

"You know now why I couldn't kill that man. Maybe I was just another soldier who was supposed to follow orders, but what would children like Nick think if their hero had become an assassin? I know that Trent had to kill, but he killed in battle against forces that were battling in return. I don't think Trent was the sort of man that could have been an assassin. I don't think he could have been a cold-blooded killer."

Julie said nothing.

"I'm so sorry, Julie. If I could trade spots with Trent, I would. I would in a heartbeat. I wish with every fiber of my being that he was standing in front of you right now, instead of me. I'd give up anything to make that happen. But even with all my abilities, there's nothing I can do to make him return."

Julie said nothing.

"I can't change the decisions that I've made. Trent is gone. If you want to think it's my fault, then I will bear that burden. I owe men like Trent that much. But, Franklin and Sophie insist that I continue to stay with them. Now that Anthem has made his official debut and they botched one attempt on my life, I don't think I need to worry about them coming back. They'll still be pursuing Freedom, but I think they'll leave Allen Hemmingway alone. I need to find out more about Walter. I need to find out more about myself, and I need to see what it's like to try to live a normal life. But I can't live next door to you, Julie, knowing that you're hating me the entire time. Please, I'm begging you, can you forgive me? I'm not saying that I want you to, um, to feel the way I thought you were starting to feel for me. I just have to know that you don't hate me. Can you tell me that?"

"Get out of my shop."

Allen turned with a tear in his eye and left Carmah's Cup.

Julie turned with a tear in her eye and went back to her pastries.

Suffocation

He'd been watching her bedroom window for what seemed like hours. In fact, as he glanced at the little watch he wore, it had actually only been about twenty minutes. He would see what he wanted; he knew it was simply a matter of patience. After all, she'd arrived home right on time. He got into position just as she was walking through her front door. He watched with anticipation as he saw the lights go on in her house as she moved from room to room. He had no idea what she did for a living, but he knew that on weeknights she got home at eleven-twenty on the dot. He could kick himself for having failed to notice sooner. However, the last week had been pure bliss. She usually didn't take more than a half-hour; he wondered how much longer it would be.

Finally, her upstairs bedroom light fired to life. He couldn't help noticing that a part of him fired to life as well. In she walked, and he could see her easily through her open blinds. She had on a blue towel tonight, he noticed. He supposed that a few days use from the white one was all she cared for. His moment of glory, near at hand, was momentarily distracted as he could have sworn he saw something from the corner of his eye moving near her back porch. Probably just a cat, he imagined. This neighborhood was wrought with them. He hated the way they always crept around in the shadows.

He couldn't worry about the cat, however, for he feared he would miss what all his hard work had been striving towards. As usual, she dropped the towel upon her bed and walked to her dresser for her sleep garb. It was only a few minutes of show, but it was worth all the patience in the world to him. He reveled as it took her a few seconds longer than usual to choose her garment, and he nearly choked with glee as she decided to admire herself in the mirror. She was a beautiful girl, he had to admit, but let's face it, it wouldn't have mattered much to him if she were beautiful or not. She was a naked girl, after all. How often did he get to see that?

He realized that time was running out as she began to dress her lower half.

Suddenly, all his joy was eradicated as he watched in horror. On the other side of her room, out of her line of vision, he saw a man lurking towards her. He didn't dare to turn his own lights on when he screamed for his father to come quickly.

"Wally, what is it?" his father demanded as he strode into Wally's bedroom. "Why do you have the lights off?"

"Leave them off!" Wally screamed in terror mixed with ashamed embarrassment. "Come look, quick!"

Paul Holzer wasn't the most moral man in town, but he couldn't help but feel disgust as he watched his fourteen-year-old son, Wally, with flaming cheeks, point out his bedroom window. It was obvious what Wally had been doing. He'd seen Becky prancing about in all her glory across the street with the blinds wide open himself, once. He hadn't stopped to watch, however. No matter how beautiful a girl is, it's just not right to be a Peepin' Tom. He would have to make sure he taught his son that lesson. Starting now.

"Boy," Paul started, "if you think you're too big for a whippin,' why you'd best think agai—"

The father suddenly stopped as he saw what it was that had turned his son milky with fear. Unbeknownst to Becky, Paul watched an intruder skulk up behind her with a plastic bag raised in the air.

"Oh my G—" Paul whispered.

"Is that him, Dad?" Wally pleaded with eyes the size of baseballs.

Paul didn't bother to answer Wally as he raced out of his son's room.

"Call the police, Janice! Tell them the killer's at Becky's house!" Paul ordered his wife as he grabbed a steak knife from the kitchen and then tore out their front door.

Moments later, Wally felt awful trepidation as he saw his father break through Becky's front door with one eye and Becky's life slip away with the other. Within instants, he watched in amazement as his father burst into Becky's bedroom to see the killer positioning her upon the bed. The killer reacted too late to Paul's entry, and, while he saw Paul sink the steak knife deep into the killer's chest, Wally felt both pride in his father and cowardice in himself for staying behind.

However, the killer could not be stopped.

He grabbed Paul by the throat and flung him across the room onto Becky's lifeless body. The killer bolted from Becky's room. Seconds later, Wally was relieved to see his father pop up and sprint after him.

The killer sprung from where Becky's front door had been before Paul smashed it in and was quickly tackled from behind after Paul caught up with him. Wally saw his father struggling with the killer and finally decided to act.

The young boy grabbed his Louisville Slugger and dashed through the house, ignoring his mother's pleas to wait for the police.

While Wally ran with all his power from his house to Becky's, he watched as the killer pulled the steak knife out of his own chest, for it had remained there since Paul had stuck it in, and raised it in the air. The killer was about to plummet it down into the dazed Paul.

Wally dashed across Becky's front lawn and cracked the killer with all his might across the back of the head with the bat his father had bought him last Christmas.

The killer fell.

Wally helped his father stand up and they looked down at the unconscious killer that was sprawled out across the lawn. Apparently, a steak knife in the chest and a bat across the head was just enough to slow him down. Paul grinned at Wally and squeezed his shoulder. Wally was in bliss.

Finally, the police arrived sans squealing sirens. Paul understood why when he saw Todd Likes get out of the squad car. Todd had lost his sister's fiancée to the monster lying upon the grass. He had made it clear without saying a word that the killer, if captured, would never see a courtroom. Most in the town of Sullen Springs had no trouble with this unspoken testimony.

"This him, Mr. Holzer?" Todd asked with a sprig of chew in his mouth.

"Yes, sir," Paul answered.

Todd walked over to the killer and looked down at him. One of Todd's officers, Don Wellscop, was still in the car, apparently radioing for people to either stay away or to hurry up, Wally couldn't determine which.

"How'd you stop him?"

"My son, Wally," Paul answered as he motioned with his head towards the boy, "clocked him in the back of the head with a bat."

"Must've been a good swing," Todd mumbled with something not quite a grin after a quick spit.

Don approached Todd and quietly said, "Alan and Austin are on their way. Tony's keeping everyone else out of it."

Todd began nodding his head and looked at Wally, "Boy, you've done a good thing tonight. You've saved countless lives here. Say," Todd began looking around, "where is Becky, anyway?"

Wally looked down and began to choke a little. "I didn't get there in time," Paul stammered.

After pressing his lips together in obvious anger and nodding to himself, Todd next turned to Don and ordered, "Have Al and Austin take care of Becky and console her parents across town." Todd next turned back to Paul and Wally. "You've come this far, fellas. You want to see it all the way through?"

Wally's eyes got big once again, "What do you mean?"

"Chief Likes," Paul corrected his son.

Blushing, Wally adapted, "What do you mean, Chief Likes?"

Todd would have been amused under ordinary circumstances at Paul's parenting, but now was not the time. "We just lost four hands with Al and Austin taking care of Becky. We need those hands for what we got planned. I need you two to help me out. It's gotta be off the record, now, so don't say you'll help if you can't keep quiet about it."

Paul answered, "God knows I'll help get this maniac out of town, but I don't want my boy involved—"

"I can help, Dad! If it hadn't been for me, we wouldn't even have caught him!"

"Oh?" Paul responded. "And you wanna tell Chief Likes how you knew the killer was in Becky's house?"

"We don't have time for this, Mr. Holzer. Can you help or not?" Todd interrupted.

Paul looked down at his son, and, after much thought, finally questioned, "What do you need us to do?"

October 26, 1961 12:07 a.m.

After making sure that Janice's sister, Carmen, had arrived to stay with her, Paul and Wally loaded into the back of Todd's squad car after stuffing the killer, tightly bound in rope and gagged, into the car's trunk.

They drove to the edge of Sullen Springs without saying a word to each other. After a long and silent ride, the three men and one boy pulled into Sullen Springs' Cemetery.

"What are we doing here?"

"You'll see, Mr. Holzer," Todd answered. "The man in the trunk is the first serial killer that Sullen Springs has ever had. We're gonna make sure that he's the last."

They drove up a large hill near the back of the cemetery to its oldest and most unfrequented region. Paul noticed that Officer Barone was leaning against his squad car smoking what was not a cigarette. Tony quickly threw the smoking object off to the side and went to the back of his own cruiser.

Todd parked his car nose to nose with Tony's and cut the engine. He and Don walked back to Tony as the latter lifted his car's trunk, obstructing the view of the three men from Wally and Paul.

"What's going on, Dad?"

"I'm not sure, son. But Chief Likes is a good man. I may not agree with much of Officer Barone, but Officer Likes has been the best thing to happen to Sullen Springs in a long time. We can trust him."

Todd, Don, and Tony suddenly reappeared. Tony had a shovel in his hand and the other two men carried two shovels apiece. Paul instantly understood Officer Likes' intentions and looked at his son.

"It's not easy sometimes, son."

Paul and Wally got out of the car and met the other three men behind it. Don and Todd handed a shovel to the father and son. Todd opened the trunk to find the killer wide-awake and still bleeding profusely from his chest wound. Tony and Don grabbed the killer by the ropes and hauled him to a bare spot on the top of the hill that they were situated upon. They dropped him in a heap in the dust while he glared hatred at them.

By the light of a full moon, the four men and Wally began digging a shallow grave.

After only a short time of efficient digging, Don and Tony stood the killer up on the edge of his final resting-place with his back to it.

"This isn't right," Wally whispered to his father.

"Now's not the time," he answered.

"But, Dad, you told me cold-blooded killin' is wrong! Isn't that what we're doing?"

Paul sighed and looked down at his son. "Wally, cold blooded killin' is wrong. If I'd killed this man in Becky's room, why, that'd be different. What we're doing is wrong, son. But I don't see no other way but this. It's the only way to rid our town of this monster. If the law don't even think we should send him to jail, well, I guess God will have to judge us as he sees fit when our time comes."

"This isn't right…" Wally whispered.

Todd slowly turned his head to Wally and scolded, "Boy, it's not right that this piece of trash has killed eight people in Sullen Springs either, now is it? This killer don't deserve due process. I'll be damned before I see some lawyer get this one off, so we're all gonna make sure that don't happen. Now you don't like it, you go off to the car and don't look. But you don't breathe a word of this to no one, hear? The town wants this fella gone, and we're gonna make sure he stays gone. Now run off to the car. You can say a prayer for your Dad and us back there. You can say a prayer for Becky, who's probably walking through the Gates right now. You can say a prayer for the other seven folks, including my would-be brother-in-law. But don't you waste one prayer of mercy on this man you see before you. He's the worst that the Devil has to offer."

The killer suddenly began to chuckle through his gag at that, and Wally began to sweat ice when his eyes locked with the killer's. Wally quickly turned and ran away from the impromptu burial.

"Take his gag off," Todd ordered. Upon completion of that task, he followed with, "Any last words before we send you on?"

The killer spit into Todd's face, and then, with just above a whisper, quite calmly snarled out, "I'm the curse of this town. Ya'll never be rid of me, understand? I'll be comin' again. I'll be comin' agai—"

"I've had enough!" Todd screamed and then shoved the killer into his shallow grave.

"I'll see you all again!" the killer roared, still bound in rope and lying face-up in his own grave. "I'll suffocate everyone in town before I'm done!"

"The only one that's suffocatin' in Sullen Springs anymore is you…" Todd muttered slowly as he reached for his shovel.

Paul, Tony, and Don followed suit and began piling dirt on the wailing killer.

January 3, 2004 4:15 p.m.

She walked into the church and was instantly unsettled by the deafening silence that attacked her. The woman looked about the room being lit by the waning sun and admired the stain glass windows along the walls. However, she hadn't come to Sullen Springs to see the sights. She began walking down the center aisle towards the altar. Just as she suspected, past the altar and around the corner, she found the Pastor's office. She knocked lightly. A small grin flashed across her face as she heard an obvious gasp of fright.

"Who is it?" an old, frightened voice called.

She opened the door to the office and saw an old pastor sitting at his desk. He was wearing a simple flannel shirt. The elderly man had a look of obvious concern written upon his face, but it quickly disappeared as he saw the attractive young woman walk through his door.

"I'm afraid I'm not taking any walk-ins today, miss," the pastor notified. "Perhaps we could arrange an appointment for later next week?"

"Father Holzer?"

"Yes?"

"I'm Lisa Keeley. You don't know me, but—"

"I do know you, young lady. Well, of you, I should say. You're Officer Barone's cousin, aren't you? Here from the city to 'substitute teach,' according to half of the town."

"You *don't* think I'm here to sub?" Lisa asked in amusement.

"I think that there are plenty of substitute teaching opportunities in the city, Ms. Keeley," Pastor Holzer assured. "If what the other half of the town says of your objective is true, I'm afraid that I certainly can't help you."

"Pastor Holzer, I'm just here as a journalist. I swear," Lisa blushed at the obvious faux pas in regards to her location, "I mean, I promise that I won't sensationalize anything. I just want to report the story in a book—period. Exactly as it happened."

The pastor looked at her with narrowed eyes and asked, "So you want to report only the past, is that it? Nothing to do with the present, hmm? Surely you have some interest in the current situation?"

"Well, now that you mention it," she began in feigned earnest, "I think that it is a rather interesting story. I would have to mention the current happenings. After all, that's what's led to the renewed interest!"

Pastor Holzer nearly became angry as he fought for control, "But there is no renewed interest unless someone publicizes the recent happenings. Ms. Keeley, Sullen Springs is very good at keeping its sins to itself. We don't want the world to know of certain things. We're known as a nice, quiet little town, and that's how we'd like to keep it. There is no connection to the past. If that's what you're thinking, I'd suggest a new approach. Now, care to tell me what led you to this so-called story?"

Lisa finally took a seat at one of the two chairs before the pastor's desk, although he did not motion for her to do so. "The recent killings have been all over the news, Pastor. Three suffocations in as many weeks. Please, this is a big story, just like it was forty-three years ago!"

"Yes," Pastor Holzer answered. "But, I know that you know more than that. Why else would you be in my church right now?"

"Well…" Lisa paused; she had already known the Pastor would put two and two together.

"Let me take a guess, as I'm something of a detective myself," the pastor sighed. "Freddy Barone told you all about what happened last month. I don't know if it was over e-mail, the phone, or what, but he told you all about it. How do I know this?" the pastor asked as he saw Lisa's eyebrows rise inquisitively. "Any male member of the Barone family can't keep his gums from flapping, that's how I know. His father couldn't keep quiet about much, so I can only presume that he told his son about things he shouldn't have. I suppose that Freddy is the reason the whole town is positive that they know who this new serial killer is."

"Well, in Freddy's defense," Lisa began for her cousin's sake, "he's nothing like his father. It's just that when your cemetery washed out in that flood a month back, he thought people should know."

"Know what?" the pastor asked, testing Lisa to see how much she did actually know.

Lisa hated being pinned into a corner, but if she were going to get an interview from this old man, she was going to have to play his game. "Look, Pastor Holzer, if I lived in Sullen Springs and there was a serial killer from forty years ago who'd been buried in an unmarked grave without the benefit of a coffin, and then the whole cemetery washed out and there wasn't a single body found that didn't match to a correlating casket, I think I'd want to know! Freddy thought it was important that the town be ready."

"Ready for what?" the pastor demanded.

"Pastor," Lisa answered, "I know that as a religious man, you probably don't believe in ghosts and zombies and things like that. However, even YOU have to admit that an empty grave washing out a month ago and a new rash of killings by suffocation breaking out within the same week is a bit more than a coincidence!"

"You think the killer has returned from the dead? Is that it?"

"You don't?"

The pastor shook his head at the young brunette wearing black-rimmed glasses and finally asked, "Why are you in my office, young lady?"

Relieved to have finally gotten to the point of her visit, she says, "It's rumored that you were the one to capture the killer four decades ago." Lisa paused as the pastor moaned in disgust and then continued, "It's also rumored that you were one of the last men to see him alive, before he apparently was put to rest in an unmarked grave."

"Really, and you heard these rumors from Officer Freddy Barone, I imagine," the pastor affirmed. "And he heard them from his father, Officer Tony Barone, who, due to a severe liking of the illegal sort, was prone to talking about things he had no business talking of."

Lisa simply nodded at the old man, knowing it was useless to try to protect her source.

"You're the only one left that I can talk with who actually saw the killer, Pastor. I won't make a fool of you, I promise."

"So, Freddy knew who was involved?"

"Well, Freddy told me that your father passed away several years ago. Freddy also said that Don Wellscop moved away several years after the killer was, er, dealt with, and that no one ever heard from him again. Uncle Tony died from an overdose about fifteen years ago. That just leaves you and Todd Likes, and he's been in a psyche ward for the last twenty years. He'd be in his seventies now, if I've got my numbers right, so I don't know how much he could remember even if he were, um, feeling well."

The pastor grunted at this last statement and responded with, "Ms. Keeley, as far as being the person to capture the killer and being the last person to see him, I can't comment on any of that. What I can tell you is that this new killer is simply a copycat, nothing more. I've always felt it was only a matter of time before someone decided to carry on that devil's work."

Lisa sighed, stood up from her chair, and stretched her still-gloved hand out to the pastor. He did not extend his, and so she thanked him anyway and turned to leave. As she walked out of his door, though, she stopped and half-turned to face him. She left him with, "Excuse me for saying so, Pastor Holzer, but if you're so certain that these latest killings are unrelated to the original, why did you sound as though you were expecting a ghost when I knocked on your door?"

January 3, 2004 10:32 p.m.

"Hello?"

"Leez?"

"Yeah. What's up, Freddy?"

"We got another killing. It happened a few hours ago. Most of the crew's takin' off; if you want to come take a look, you can. If you see another cruiser besides mine, though, don't stop."

Lisa grabbed a pen and paper. "Thanks a ton, Freddy! Where are you?"

January 3, 2004 10:49 p.m.

Lisa rolled up to the spot. She saw Freddy's cruiser sitting alone with the lights flashing, but there was no siren. She pulled up behind him on the old dirt road. She could see Freddy's head in his car before he started to get out.

"Find it okay?" Freddy asked.

"Yeah, but talk about being out in the middle of nowhere!"

"Well, you think that about Sullen Springs whether you're in the country or not!" Freddy teased. "Come on, you're about to be in the middle of nowhere's nowhere. You'll see why in a second."

Lisa followed Freddy as he turned on his flashlight and walked off the dirt road onto a path leading between two cornfields. The corn was down, but you still couldn't see a thing out here unless you knew exactly where you were going. Apparently, someone did, for Lisa saw a newer model Grand Prix parked a few meters ahead. She instantly noticed when Freddy shined his flashlight on the car that the driver's side window had been shattered and that the passenger door was wide open.

"Lilard and Swoke will be back in a bit to secure the crime scene. The three of us just came to check it out when we found this. A lot more than we bargained for. Anyway, you've gotta hurry, they'll be back any minute. I could get in a lot of trouble for lettin' you know about this."

Lisa pecked Freddy on the side of the face and smiled as his cheeks flushed in the thirty-degree weather. "I appreciate it, Freddy. Mind if I check it out?"

"Just don't touch anything, Leez. Eyes only, 'kay?"

"Oka—Oh, my God! Freddy!" Lisa yelled upon looking into the Grand Prix, "There's a body in here!"

Freddy walked up behind her. "I know. The coroner ain't gotten here yet. That's why I told you to see what you want and then get out of here!"

Lisa suddenly understood the urgency she'd noted in Freddy's voice and took out her mini-recorder.

"Hey," Freddy interrupted before she could turn it on, "I'm off the record here, so you want to ask me anything, you do it now!"

Lisa made a sour face at her cousin and put the recorder back into her pea coat. "How'd you know to find the scene way out here in the boonies?"

"Old Mr. Baer saw some kids driving down the dirt road past his place. He knew that people used his property as a make-out spot, so he wanted us to run them off. I radioed Lilard and Swoke to meet me here so we could <ahem!> catch them in the act, you know? Anyway, we got more than we bargained for."

"So these are kids?" Lisa asked as she poked her head through the broken glass. The driver was a male, she could see that much, but the garbage bag wrapped around his head obstructed the view of his identity. "Who's the driver? Where's his make-out buddy?"

Freddy thrust his head to the left and said, "She's off yonder. It's Trish Finley and George Prochnow—"

"Oh, no," Lisa whispered. "I had them in class yesterday!"

Freddy nodded his head slowly. "Both seniors. We figure that the killer broke out George's window and put the bag over his head. Looks like Trish tried to make a run for it, but she got bagged about a hundred meters out."

Lisa furrowed her brow in contemplation before offering, "How'd the killer catch up to her so quickly? He couldn't have suffocated George in the time it would take Trish to run a hundred meters!"

Freddy's eyes lit up and then his cheeks flushed in embarrassment once more. It was fairly obvious to Lisa that three of Sullen Springs' finest had not yet made this deduction.

"Um, I'm not sure," Freddy stuttered.

"Should we look for footprints?" Lisa asked.

Freddy whacked himself alarmingly hard in the head with his flashlight. "Damn it!" he yelled out loud. "We contaminated the scene already when we walked over to Trish's body. With the ground being as hard as it is, along with it being darker than a squirrel's butthole out here, and the three of us traipsing around, I don't know if we'll find anything."

"Let's have a look anyway, want to?" Lisa asked.

Suddenly, about a mile away, Lisa and Freddy saw two different pairs of headlights approaching them.

"You gotta go now, Leez! That's Lilard and Swoke coming back with the gear. We'll see if we can't find anything new, but you gotta move!"

January 4th, 2004 9:52 a.m.

Sullen Springs High School was connected to Sullen Springs Junior High. Sullen Springs Junior High was connected to Sullen Springs Elementary. Needless to say, Lisa's graduating class of 1996 would have filled up all three of these phases. There were several aspects of small town life that Lisa couldn't get use to. One, as already made obvious, was the very small schools. Another was the fact that there was only one place that delivered dinner, and that was only if you liked cardboard pizza. A third, although she very much wished she could join them, was the fact that the whole town was in one of four churches at this time of day every Sunday. She'd never been a church going gal, however, so instead of sitting in Pastor Holzer's congregation, she was pulling into the Sullen Springs' High School/Junior High/Elementary parking lot.

Lisa had replaced the first of the new killer's victims, an old history teacher that everyone called Widow Wellscop. Lisa heard that she wasn't truly a widow, but ever since her husband, Don, had disappeared years and years ago, they just treated her as though her husband had died.

While Lisa had a Master's in Journalism, she could still substitute teach any subject. It was just a way to pay the bills during her temporary relocation and to keep a finger on the pulse of town. Anything that was worth knowing around here you'd pick up either in the halls or the faculty lounge of Sullen Springs High School.

Lisa needed to get some work done for the coming week, no matter how lightly she took her history teaching gig. She figured if she got it done in the morning, she could focus the rest of her day on finding more information on the old and the new killer, and perhaps a possible connection between them. She still had hours before the last of the churchgoers got home.

"Well, looks like I'm not the only one getting some work done," Lisa commented to herself as she noticed that Principal Delorenzo's Liberty was in the lot. She pulled up next to it, since it was parked closest to the front doors, and then used her keys to enter the old school.

Lisa thought for a moment about swinging past the office to say hello to Principal Delorenzo, but she didn't care too much for the administrator. She got the feeling that Delorenzo didn't care too much for her as well. Small town folks usually don't like big city outsiders coming in to stir things up. Even the pastors of the towns aren't the friendliest folks. Lisa couldn't say she blamed them much, however. After all, she was using Sullen Springs as a rung on her ladder to success.

January 4, 2004 11:09 a.m.

Finally finished with her lesson plans for the week (she only had two preps, after all), Lisa began to load up her bag. Suddenly, from the corner of her eye, she caught Mr. Zehr's Accord pulling into the lot. Mr. Zehr was a math teacher around Lisa's age. He was very friendly with Lisa and she had actually considered asking him over for some cardboard pizza one of these nights. Next to the forty-three-year-old Principal Delorenzo, Mr. Zehr was the only person that worked in the school that was even close to Lisa's tender age of twenty-six.

"He must be here to get some work done as well," Lisa mumbled to herself. "Maybe I'll stop by his room on my way ou—"

Lisa stopped in mid-sentence as she saw Principal Delorenzo quickly jump out of Zehr's car. Mr. Zehr hastily drove away one direction, and Principal Delorenzo drove off in the other.

"That's odd," Lisa said out loud.

January 4, 2004 3:24 p.m.

"Hello?" Lisa answered.

"Leez?"

"Yes, Freddy. It's always me. Who else would answer my cell?"

Lisa snickered at the incomprehensible muttering she barely heard from the other end. "What do you want, Freddy?" she asked with good nature.

"I wanted to know if you wanted to grab some dinner tonight? I was thinking of ordering pizza."

Lisa pulled her car into the nursing home's parking lot. "Sure, Freddy. What time?" Lisa began nodding her head when she heard Freddy tell her around six-thirty. "Sounds good." She continued to listen to her cousin as she finished parking her car into one of many open spots. She then answered, "No, I've had no luck at all today. No one will talk to me. I've gotten so desperate, I'm at the nursing home to talk with Todd Likes...Yes, I know he's in the psyche ward, but he's the only person left who hasn't turned me away! By the way, Freddy," she began, "what's the connection between Doug Zehr and Principal Delorenzo?...Yes, I know that they work together, I work with them as well, remember?...Nothing that you know of, huh? Okay, well, I gotta go. I'll see you tonight...Right, okay. I'll bring the beer. Bye."

January 4, 2004 3:28 p.m.

Lisa entered the home and tried to ignore all of the old, decrepit people that reached out to touch her as she walked through the halls. She was more than unnerved as they begged for her to take them with her. Lisa was not very good at dealing with situations such as this, so she chose to ignore them and bolt to the front desk.

"Hi," Lisa offered to the front desk worker. "Could you tell me which room Todd Likes is in?"

The front desk worker whose name was Anne, according to her nametag, eyed Lisa over rather rudely and spat out, "Are you relation?"

"Um, no," Lisa hesitated. She feared that this would happen. After all, it's not like you can just waltz into a psyche ward. She had hoped that these small town country folks wouldn't be quite as stringent.

"If you're not relation, you can't see him. Besides, he's no longer here anyway."

"What do you mean?"

"I'm afraid that it's none of your business, Ms. Keeley, isn't it?" Anne's superior suddenly said after having appeared.

January 4, 2004 6:42 p.m.

Lisa and Freddy sat in his living room on the floor while watching some old reruns and eating the best pizza in town. Lisa detested it. They'd downed two beers waiting for the pizza to be delivered.

"I swear, Leez, I told you weeks ago at the family reunion not to come to Sullen Springs, didn't I? I knew you'd get nowhere with these folks. They just don't take to your kind!"

"You mean educated, sophisticated, ambitious city girls on their way up?"

"No, I mean snobby women looking to cash in on other people's problems."

Lisa threw a pepperoni at her cousin from across the coffee table. She knew it was just a joke mixed with a bit of the beer-truth, but it still hurt her feelings a little.

"Well, I hate to support the stereotype, but I have a few more things I need to know."

Freddy nearly spit out the beer he had up to his lips. After gaining control once more, he quickly slurred out through half-swallowed alcohol, "You never stop! By golly!"

"Come on, Freddy! Just one question, please!" she begged.

Freddy slammed his beer bottle down on the table and growled, "What?"

"What happened to Todd Likes?"

"I knew that was going to be it!" Freddy laughed out.

"Do you have an answer?" Lisa demanded.

"I don't have a definite answer, no."

"But you have something," she prodded.

"I swear, girl, sometimes I can't believe we got the same blood flowin' through our veins!"

"So you DO have something!" she smiled.

Freddy shook his head and answered, "Neolithic Nurse Knabbery, who was old when my dad was a kid, swears that she saw someone break Likes out through his window. She says she walked in to give him his medicine last night, and there was an old man lifting him right out the darn window!"

"Do you believe it?" Lisa interrogated.

"Well, Knabbery's older than dirt, but she's still more right in the head than most of the town. I think I probably do believe her. Likes *is* gone, after all."

"So he was kidnapped?"

"Ha! No, we're not treating it as a kidnapping."

"Why?"

"Well, Likes is no kid, first of all. Second, most the town thinks that it was more of a rescue than anything."

"A rescue?" Lisa asked in disbelief. "Who rescued him from what?"

Freddy took a long swig from his beer before laughing out, "Knabbery swears that it was a much older version of Don Wellscop that busted Likes out. Most people figure that if it is the original killer, Likes would be on his list. Guess old Wellscop was still alive after all. He must've come to rescue his old chief!"

"So where'd they go?"

"Who knows? Maybe they're hiding in the country somewhere between here and Kithlessville. Hard to tell. We're not out looking for them, if that's what you're getting at."

Suddenly, the phone rang. Freddy shot up and trotted to his kitchen, leaving Lisa to her thoughts. After a few moments of sipping on her third beer, a weather alert interrupted an old episode of her least favorite show that she was watching. It warned that they were going to get a very heavy snow tonight and to stay off the roads if at all possible. Freddy returned.

"How you feelin'?" Freddy asked.

"What do you mean?"

"I mean are you sober enough to go out?"

"I guess. Why?"

"Wally Holzer was just found dead in his church parking lot."

January 4, 2004 7:12 p.m.

"Thanks for calling us, Tim," Freddy said to Officer Lilard.

Lilard smirked at Freddy and answered, "Just make it quick. You're off duty, I can smell beer on your breath, and you've got a civilian with you that half the town hates."

Lisa's eyebrows shot up in disbelief upon hearing Lilard's last statement. She knew that she wasn't looked upon fondly, but half the town hated her! That was news! Was a possible best-selling-factually-accurate-book-about-a-killer-returned-from-the-dead really worth a whole town hating her forever? Yes, she thought it probably was.

"Can we see Pastor Holzer?" Lisa asked Officer Lilard, trying to sound sweet.

"He's next to his car, around the corner," Lilard informed. "Make sure she don't touch anything, Freddy."

Lisa and Freddy quickly strode around the back corner of the church and saw Pastor Holzer sprawled out across his hood with the usual garbage bag wrapped around his head. Lisa was having a difficult time accepting the fact that she had patronized this man only a day before about fearing for his life.

Lisa took out her tape recorder and began making notes for later. Freddy drew an invisible zipper across his mouth as soon as he saw the tape recorder go out, and he remained silent until it was turned off and put back into her pocket.

"What do you think?" she asked her cousin now that everything was off the record.

"I think that the chief is going to be up in arms. Holzer was his pastor. It's just like with Likes forty years ago. This'll probably be the straw that broke the camel's back. My guess is, the killer can look forward to another shallow grave."

"Freddy, do you really think a killer returned from the dead has any fear of anything that your police department might do to him?"

"It's not a killer returned from the dead, Leez. It's just some copycat, that's all."

Lisa and Freddy began walking away from Pastor Holzer's body and back to their own car. Lisa called out thanks to Lilard and he grunted at her in return. Freddy explained that Lisa should consider her one favor owed for pointing out that Trish couldn't have been killed by suffocation the same moment as George Prochnow from a hundred meters away paid in full.

"What is your explanation for that, anyway?" Lisa asked Freddy as they noticed a heavy snow beginning to fall.

Freddy simply shook his head and said they were working on it. They returned back to Freddy's house and finished eating their pizza.

January 5, 2004 6:22 a.m.

"I am so glad that we got snowed in together," Doug Zehr affirmed.

"Me too," Principal Delorenzo answered. "It's especially sweet considering Dale's on business across the country for three more days. That means we'll have more of this morning for the next seventy-two hours."

Regina Delorenzo crawled out of bed without bothering to cover up. Doug watched with an admiring eye as she walked into the bathroom and began to pull her hair back into a ponytail. Most women felt that long hair was no longer appropriate once they hit their forties. Doug was quite glad that Regina was not one of those women.

"It's working, isn't it?" Doug said with a smile to her.

"Why wouldn't it? Once we found the body that night, we knew this town would fall all over itself to believe that the killer had returned. A few random victims, a few strategic victims, it's child's play when dealing with Sullen Springs. Just a few more, then we sit tight for the rest of the year and get the hell out of this nowhere-ville by mid-June."

"Dale will be easy, but how are we going to take care of Keeley?"

"I don't know, Doug. We've got to do it, though. I swear I saw her looking at us yesterday morning when you dropped me off. If she tells her cousin about us, even that idiot might put two and two together. Even a Barone could figure it out if they thought about it long enough. Take her out of the picture and Barone will be too preoccupied with her death. It's no secret how he feels about her."

"And your dad?"

"He'll call eventually. Crazy as he is, he'll call and tell me where we can find him. Don did us the biggest favor of all. Old fool. We'll get rid of those two last. It'll look like the "returned killer" will have fulfilled his graveside promise. It'll all work out perfectly!"

"You sure you're his only heiress in the will?" Doug asked his still-nude lover as she was washing her face.

Regina put her washrag down and walked over to the bed, sitting next to Doug. She began stroking his cheek before offering, "The money's ours, Doug. That old woman left it to Dad for having the guts to take care of the killer forty years ago. He was too cheap to ever use it, so he put it away. Now, as soon as his body's found, I'll get it all and we'll start our lives together. You'll leave at the end of the school year for a new job down south, I'll inevitably have to give up my job due to intolerable grieving for the death of my father, and the money will be all ours. We'll even get a nice little bonus from Dale's death."

"Fool-proof," Doug whispered.

"As long as we can't be connected to the killings. Have you gotten rid of it yet?"

"Regina, I told you, I can't do it alone! He's too damn heavy, even if he has been buried for forty years. What's his deal, anyway? Shouldn't he just be a skeleton by now?"

"I don't know, Doug, but if they find that body in your basement, we can kiss all of our plans goodbye! You've got to get rid of it!"

"Say when you can help, and we'll do it!" he exclaimed.

"I guess we'll wrap him up and stuff him in the back of the Liberty today. Should we still meet on the hill?"

"Yep," Doug answered. "We'll dig him a new hole just a few meters away from his original, re-cover him with dirt and snow, and people will think that he just didn't wash all the way out during the flood."

"I'm glad we picked the cemetery that night for our rendezvous," Regina crooned.

"Me too, baby. Why don't you get back into bed for a few minutes?" Doug asked as he pulled the sheets aside.

"No time, Doug," Regina answered. "I still need to make an appearance at the school, snowed out or not! I'm going to hop in the shower…"

Doug groaned as he watched his illicit lover walk away and close the bathroom door. He reached for the remote and turned on the morning news as he continued to lie naked in bed.

January 6, 2004 8:58 p.m.

Freddy banged on Lisa's front door. The snow had melted a little, but not enough for most folks to brave the outdoors. Thanks to his snowmobile he kept in the back shed, however, snow was of no matter to him. He knew that Lisa didn't keep squat around the house in the way of food, so he thought he'd bring her a little chicken he had fried up, along, of course, with all the fixin's! It'd be a tremendous help, consequently, if she'd just open the front door so he could stop freezing his badge off!

"Leez!" he screamed through the door. "It's freakin' cold out here! Open up!" Freddy emphasized his shouts by pushing the doorbell continuously for several minutes.

It's no mystery that the Sullen Springs Police Department has been considered a tad inept since Chief Likes left some years ago, but even Freddy Barone can make sound deductions every once in a while. Lisa's lights were on, but she's not answering the door. He'd given her enough time to get off the pot. He'd given her enough time to get out of the shower and put on a robe. He couldn't hear a stereo or TV blaring through the walls of her little two-bedroom rental house. Obviously, as far as Freddy was concerned, something was wrong.

He kicked in the front door.

Although he didn't have a gun on him since he was off duty, Freddy nevertheless charged headfirst through the house. He started in the living room, then went straight into the kitchen. He grabbed a kitchen knife, just to be on the safe side, and his heart fell as he saw that Lisa's back door was ajar. There was a puddle of water where snow had blown in and melted. Freddy looked down and saw something he had missed before. Wet footprints that were neither his nor Lisa's. They led toward the bedrooms.

Freddy sped past the bathroom at full speed, glanced into the room that Lisa actually slept in, saw nothing, and sprinted to the other bedroom that she used as an office.

She was slumped over her laptop with a garbage bag wrapped around her head.

Freddy screamed in anguish and ripped the bag from his precious cousin. It was too late. She was already purple.

Freddy fell onto Lisa's desk in a heap, knocking all of its contents to the floor, along with Lisa and himself. In the havoc of the landslide from the desk, Lisa's mini-recorder came to life and he heard his cousin's last recording.

"January 5th, 2004. Around eleven-forty. I thought that Freddy was a genius. After we went back to his place from observing the pastor's crime scene, we had a few more beers then bounced around his theory of how Trish Finley had been killed the same moment as George Prochnow. It's so simple!

"There are two killers! Freddy said that there's no way, ghost or not, that someone could suffocate an eighteen-year-old boy then catch a seventeen-year-old girl within a hundred meters and suffocate her as well. It defied all logic, no matter how supernatural the case may be. Freddy decided that there must be two very much alive killers, and that they were using the legend of the original killer to freak everyone out.

"It made perfect sense to me, so we started brainstorming who the killers could be. I thought that it might be Likes and Wellscop, since they had an obvious connection to the original killer and were both considered a little off their rocker.

"Freddy disagreed. He reminded me about when I had asked him what the connection was between Zehr and Delorenzo. He thought that the two might be having an affair. If that were the case, wouldn't it be a great alibi for them if the original killer returned and took care of her father and husband!

"I told Freddy that I didn't follow his logic, so he explained to me that his dad had leaked to him in one of his many intoxicated states that Likes was a millionaire now due to money being left to him from some lady in town. Since Principal Delorenzo was his only surviving relative, that money was due to her upon his death.

"Now, Freddy asked me to imagine that I was Delorenzo and that I was having an affair with a much younger man. How else could I get rid of my husband, get my dad's money, and the two of us disappear without a care in the world?

"It made perfect sense. I told Freddy that I thought he was a genius, then I must have passed out because I woke up the next morning on his couch with a pillow and blanket.

"I was having a bowl of cereal when Freddy burst in through his back door and said he had gotten a warrant for the arrest of Delorenzo and Zehr. He told me that his chief didn't care how circumstantial the evidence was, they were going to get an answer that day as to who the killer was!

"Freddy and I got on his snowmobile and rode over to Zehr's house. We met Swoke there. Lilard and Chief Williams were going to Delorenzo's place.

"We searched the first floor. Found nothing. Then we moved to the second floor. Poor Freddy. He was beside himself, as was I, honestly. It would have been a great ending to the story, and Freddy would have definitely been the hero. I guess it just wasn't in the cards. We were back at square one.

"Freddy was dead-on about Delorenzo and Zehr's affair. Everything else, though, was completely wrong. Doug was lying naked in his bed with a garbage bag wrapped around his head. Freddy figured that there had been some kind of a struggle, then he had been placed on the bed. Principal Delorenzo was in the bathroom with the water running, one leg in the shower, the rest of her sprawled out on the floor.

"Swoke said he found a bunch of dried mud on an old worktable in Zehr's basement, and not much else. Too bad. I really thought Freddy had this one in the bag, no pun intended.

"Oh, well. It's been a busy day and I think it's about time for bed. No school tomorrow, they've already decided that. I think I'll start writing the book tomorrow sometime. Even though I don't have an ending yet, I can easily get it started."

Freddy reached out to the mini-recorder and turned it off. With tears in his eyes and shaking uncontrollably, he began to stumble to the kitchen to call an ambulance. Even in shock, he knew it was useless, but he would do it anyway. He walked into the kitchen and picked up the phone.

Too late he noticed the back door was now shut.

Too late he realized a garbage bag had been thrown over his head.

The Runner

His name was Tartar, and although this inclined people to forever associate him with being fishy, he preferred to think of it as the only line of Shakespeare he had bothered to memorize, "…swifter than arrow from Tartar's bow." That was his obsession, after all—swiftness. It's what he had been working at for thirteen weeks now. And now, on this last day of his thirteenth week, Ryan Tartar was almost only a mile from being mid-way through his twenty mile run.

The soles of his running shoes baked with each stride the twenty-nine-year-old took on the old, rundown highway. He thought little of his slight body weight crashing down with three times its usual force with each step, and instead focused on the abandoned dirt road to his left where he will run his tenth and eleventh mile.

In the old days, Ryan always had to calculate the mileage in his head, which was a terrible nuisance for him as he was not inclined towards mathematics. Thankfully, his wife had been thoughtful enough to buy him a GPS sports watch. This meant his calculating days were over, now the only mental taxation was to look at the display strapped to his wrist and register how far he had gone and how much further he must go.

Little clouds of dust spit up behind the runner's feet as he propelled forward, desperately intent upon maintaining his ideal pace. If he thought the first ten were difficult, the last ten would be murderous. In order to run the twenty-six point two miles five weeks from now within the time he hoped for, it was imperative that he ran his last ten miles faster than the first. His spirit was strong and his body was primed. Nothing would keep him from his goal.

Ten miles exactly. Time to turn around and crank out the next ten. The hazel-eyed man stopped so abruptly he almost blew out both of his knees.

It had been in his line of vision for the last quarter mile, ever since he came over the top of the little bluff. There it was, off to his right as he ran between the two wild fields that either no one claimed or someone had neglected for at least half a century. A little barn. It might have been painted at one point in time, but now it simply appeared as old, rotting wood.

Ryan Tartar stood stupidly, staring straight ahead with the taciturn barn to his right. He was completely unaware of the sweat rolling down his scalp, giving his face and neck a salty shower. The singlet he wore, even though it was designed to whisk away sweat, was drenched. Somewhere, deep within his subconscious, a voice was pleading with him to begin running again. It did not do so out of concern for making good time.

It was calling to him. With a voice that not the most sensitive of machinery could ever detect, the barn was calling the runner.

The tall grass gently scratched his bare legs up to the quadriceps as he slid toward the decrepit structure. Through the cracks in the old slabs of wood that made up the doors, Ryan could just barely make out something within the ancient edifice. He pulled on the doors. They fell slowly towards him and he had to scurry back several feet to keep from being buried beneath them.

Once the dust had cleared, a pair of glistening eyes suddenly seized the runner's. It was a crow that, once having realized that Ryan had accepted its existence, flew with a whoosh through the top of the dilapidated building.

It was what the crow had been perched atop that made Ryan's mind burn. He slowly approached it. How long had it been in this barn? Years? Certainly. Decades? Assuredly. It was of a model so old that Ryan couldn't begin to guess its make. It had to have been black, once. Now it was more rust than anything, thanks to the barn whose emaciated roof served as little shelter from the rain and snow. As he neared, the breathing of the athlete grew even heavier than before, and the sweat was no longer just rolling from his body, it was now coming down in torrents.

A sedan. That's what it was. He may not know the exact make and model, but he could certainly tell that it was a sedan, even as he approached it from behind. Although it had a rusted body with dirt caked upon its exterior, it was still a marvel for Ryan to have beheld. The only question was the one of why it was turning his blood to ice and his stomach to fire?

The runner was close enough now to touch it, but he dared not do so with the sun peeking at him perversely through the cracks of the barn. Whoever had parked this antique had left the widows down; he could see that now as he walked beside it on the driver's side. He stuck his head through the window and nearly lost his nose!

He was deafened momentarily by the vicious barks of a coyote that he had awakened as it snapped at him. Ryan fell backwards onto his side and then saw the coyote bolt through a rusted-out hole in the floorboard. It scurried away and squeezed between the boards of the barn.

Had he urinated upon himself? He thought he had, but it turned out to simply be the sweat soaking through his running shorts. As he stood back up, he should have been annoyed at the dirt, dust, and grime that had stuck to his soaking skin. He was not. He simply did what he had done before, again, with no regard to his nose. He poked his head back through the window.

He saw decades of nature within the confines of the black sedan as he peered into the back seat and began to sweep his eyes over the terrain until coming upon the front passenger seat. Without much thought at all, he next peered from the passenger's seat to the driver's seat, settled upon the gearshift a moment, then moved on to the steering wheel. Needless to say, the innards of this fossil had little in common with his '04 SUV.

It was on the dash of the automobile that something had further caused Ryan a zealous, though inexplicable, need to know of it. It was a book. It appeared to be a book as old as the car, if not older! That title…he had heard of it somewhere. Suddenly, it clicked with the man whose interest in books was only superceded by his interest in mathematics. His junior year in high school he had read that book—*The Great Gatsby*. It had something to do with "The Blues Age," as he inaccurately recalled.

The runner suddenly realized that something was wrong with the nearly shredded book. It appeared as though it was faintly rusted—just like the sedan. Ryan thought that this was odd. Science was something that he was quite good at, and he had yet to examine a book capable of rust.

It was at this very moment that the would-be marathoner's throat began to close and his hands went numb. His eyes had been scanning upward from the dash as he tried to recall where he knew that book from, and they settled upon a horror. It couldn't be!

As the primordial section of his brain screamed a cautionary warning to the man, he reached out anyway and touched the black sedan. A hypothesis had been made, and it was time to prove its validity.

The door-handle pulled easily, easier than it should have, and the door swung open without a sound. Logic dictated that a car covered in rust was incapable of silence when forced to move. Logic was no longer residing in the old barn.

Ryan stepped onto the running board and climbed in. He had been right. What he saw was directly in front of his face. It could be nothing else.

The bullet hole in the windshield miraculously began to close. Ryan started to reach out to touch it, but his arm was suddenly caught tightly. With super-human speed, Ryan shot his eyes to whatever it was that was holding his right wrist. Within the span of less than the one-hundredth of a second that it took his eyes to move from the shrinking bullet hole to the vice upon his arm, he registered that the old copy by F. Scott Fitzgerald now appeared to be nearly brand new.

After an eternity had been spent in that one-hundredth of a second, Ryan settled his sight upon a black-gloved hand popping out from a black wool sleeve.

"We told you to shut off the Black Hawk!" a voice yelled from his right over the thundering of a powerful engine.

"Whaddya gonna do, read adda a dime like dis?" another voice mocked from behind.

Ryan's eyes shot from the gloved hand seizing his wrist, up and through the now fully intact windshield of the car, noticed quicker than lightning that he saw the inside of a newly constructed barn, and then fired his gaze to where the voice next to him had come from.

"Face forward and cut the engine, Franklin! I don't want to tell you again!" the man next to him commanded. Ryan saw a man with brown eyes staring into his own. This man wore a hat and suit like those that had been hugely popular in the late 1990's when Swing music had come back.

"Turn idoff!" the ignorant sounding voice yelled into his ear from behind.

Once the iron claw had been withdrawn, Ryan reached out and turned the key within the ignition. He noticed that his formerly bare arm was now cov-ered with the same sort of sleeve as his apparent passenger. In fact, as he glanced down, he saw that he too was dressed as though he were going Swing dancing with his wife. The thunder ceased. The silence was maddening.

"Whaddis id wid fella's like yous anyways, huh, Frankie?" the voice from behind began. Ryan glanced into the rear view mirror and was met, astound-ingly, with another pair of brown eyes that were no longer hazel. Then he saw the man behind himself, who also had brown eyes. The man in the rear sported a thin moustache that did nothing to hide his garish looks. The grating voice of the rear passenger continued, "When Da Boss says something, ya lisen! Na yous, dough! Yous like Weiss, who dought he could mess wid Da Boss!

What Da Boss did do Weiss last year shoulda tot ya do know bedder! Da Boss god Weiss, jus like he god O'banion, jus like he gid evrybody."

"What Mr. Adelberto is saying, Franklin, is that Mr. Capone would have taken care of your problem within a matter of time," the man to Ryan's right began. "As a gesture of goodwill and commitment towards your dilemma, he replaced your Packard with this brand new Stutz…"

"Dwo hundrid nindey-eighd cubic inch, straighd-eighd, wid one hundridden horsepowa! Ya god some nerve, Frankie, dodo Da Boss like ya done…" Mr. Adelberto chastised.

"I think that there's some mistake," Ryan began as his mind could not even begin to conceive of how he had been placed within this situation.

"There's no mistake," the man to Ryan's right began as he gently placed his forefinger upon Ryan's cheek, adjusting it so that the athlete's eyes faced forward towards the disappeared bullet hole once more after Ryan had attempted to steal a glance at him. "We understand that you are distraught over Benjamin's death. We understand that you need revenge. It was coming, Franklin. Your father's death would not have been in vain. But," he continued, "Mr. Capone was waiting for the right opportunity. Mr. Moran will make a mistake sooner or later. When that happens, Mr. Capone will take down Mr. Moran, and so too then will fall your father's killer, Mr. Stout."

"We know ya wanad da kill Slinky Sdoud, Frankie. Bud ya shoulda waided for id do be don righd. Dryin' do turnim in doda cops, na good…"

"Omerta," the man to Ryan's right said. "You forgot it, didn't you. Or perhaps you didn't care."

"I'm just a runner…" Ryan squeaked out with panic in his voice.

"That's right," the man to his right said. "One of Mr. Capone's best. You were with Mr. Torrio until he left Mr. Capone solely in charge, and now you're with Mr. Capone. You've been one of the best since Mr. Volstead and the Women's Christian Temperance Union decided to put us in business seven years ago. But, you're still only a runner. A dime a dozen. And a runner does what Mr. Capone says, and nothing else."

Ryan started to turn his head in puzzlement and look at the man to his right, but he felt the gentle forefinger guide his cheek so that he only looked straight ahead once more. Ryan's eyes bolted from the spot where the bullet hole had been, down to the book on the dash, and back to the previously damaged windshield.

"I prefer Conrad, myself," the man to his right said in regards to Franklin's choice of reading. As he said this, the location of the voice altered just enough so that Ryan could sense the man to his right had looked back to the man sitting behind the runner.

Ryan heard from behind his head what he imagined could only have been a revolver preparing to fire.

The door to the rusted black sedan flew open as Ryan fell in a heap to the dirty, dusty, grimy ground below.

He flew to his feet and ran the fastest ten miles of his life.

Severed Wires

The northeast corner of the backyard had been retooled more times than Doug's Saturday night programs. When he and Kay had first moved into the old, two-story at 10 Woodson Drive, it had simply been a patch of grass with bushes lining the neighbor's chain-linked fence. For a while there was a sandbox on it, next to the bushes, and that's where their son had always played when he was little. As the years passed, the sandbox was discarded, and it went back to being a simple patch of grass. More years passed, the neighbors put up a tall wooden fence to replace the chain-link one, and Kay began planting flowers around the bushes. The northeast part of the backyard was now a garden of beautiful flowers and birdhouses so lush that the bushes were nearly engulfed. But, it was always a work in progress, and there was more work to be done.

Doug had already dug the holes he would place the little white decorative fence posts in. It was just a large enough fence to cover the northeast corner of the northeast corner, if that makes sense. It was purely for looks, it had no function whatsoever. Ah, but it would look good! There was just one small problem as Doug saw it. Those holes, they needed to be just a little deeper. Maybe an inch or so. Doug headed back for his digger. After all, if you're going to do something, it should be done right.

"Doug, what are you doing?" Kay asked through the kitchen window screen as Doug jigged by.

"I think the holes need to be a bit deeper, dearest," he replied without losing a step.

Kay began to chuckle before she teased, "Doug, you were fine with the holes yesterday! We have dinner tonight with the Summerhaven's. Let's just put the fence in so you can help me get the house ready."

Doug stopped abruptly and looked at her through the mesh of the screen. He had a trait in which his mouth would hang open incredulously whenever a wave of disbelief would come over him.

"Just put the fence in? Kay, it'll be too high if I put it in right now!"

"Things don't always have to look perfect…" Kay sang cheerily.

"I'm afraid that they do, Kay. If you haven't figured that out about me in all this time, well then, I think you may have had a man on the side!"

"Why not a woman?" Kay deadpanned.

And with that, Doug huffed and walked away, headed around the house for the garage. He found his old trusty digger right where he had left it not twenty-four hours before and headed back to the northeast corner of the backyard.

He paid no attention to the phone ringing while he stalked past the kitchen window. It did not register with Doug at all that Kay was having a wonderful conversation within moments of the phone being answered.

Whump! The digger drove into the dirt like a hot-bladed dagger, and Doug pulled out the excess. Hole one—perfectly ready.

"Doug!" Kay called from inside the kitchen. "Your son would like to talk to you!"

Whump! A quick jab, an easy pull. Hole two—perfectly ready.

"Doug, stop what you're doing and come talk to your son," Kay yelled with a touch of anger in her voice.

Doug raised the digger high into the air and prepared for the third and final plunge. "I'll talk with him later, Kay! I'm not finished with this job yet!"

Whump! Hole three—perfectly rea-…oh, no.

He bent over and examined the new hole. He lifted his glasses up a hair as he peered below them and saw what he did not want to see. A wire…severed.

"Doug, you stubborn old man!" Kay hissed as she stormed toward him. "Do you realize that our son was calling to tell you some great news and you wouldn't give him the time of day! You upset him so much he hung up!"

Doug seemed to think a moment and then looked at Kay and asked without surprise, "He hung up?"

"You haven't spoken to him in years, Doug. I'm surprised he bothers to call anymore at all," Kay answered.

Doug grunted, then looked back down to the severed wire.

"Can you tell me what is so important in that hole that it was worth Chris hanging up on me?"

"Try calling someone," Doug requested nervously.

"Like our only child, maybe," Kay mumbled as she lifted up the cordless phone. A few moments of perplexity passed, then she informed, "There's no dial tone…"

Doug's shoulders slumped while he moaned under his breath, "Crap."

"What is it?"

"Honey," Doug muttered in embarrassment while still staring down into his hole, "I think I messed up."

Kay's eyes began to well up and a wide smile spread across her face, "You're finally going to make up with Chris!"

He snapped his eyes in an instant at Kay and answered simply, "Run over to Rollings next door and see if you can use their phone."

Kay couldn't meet Doug's eyes. "This has nothing to do with you feeling any remorse about Chris hanging up on us, does it?"

"I don't think he hung up on us. I think I hung up on him," Doug replied.

Kay turned and walked away from her husband of forty-two years.

Doug looked at the severed wire and couldn't believe he'd been so stupid.

After ten minutes, Kay returned to find Doug sitting next to his hole in the ground working on an iced tea. She did not look happy.

"What did you do this time, Doug?" she asked.

"Rollings' phone dead?"

"Um, yeah," she sarcastically answered. "And the phone is also dead at the Moores, the Bradys, the Sankaands, and the Widills. All the houses on our street have no working phones. Now, what did you do?"

Doug sat up and dusted off the seat of his old jeans. "I cut through an underground phone line. I was hoping it was just our house, but…"

"So Chris didn't hang up on us!"

Doug just shook his head in disbelief. He thought it was rather obvious that they had more pressing concerns at the moment than being hung up on.

"Kay, do you love me?" he asked timidly.

"Of course, Doug."

"Then I need you to do something for me that I can't bear to do myself."

A glimmer of hope entered Kay's eyes and she said wishfully, "Name it."

Doug took a long sip from his tea and then voiced, "Go to all of the neighbors again and tell them your idiot husband cut the phone line on accident. If they need to make a call, they are more than welcome to come use our cell."

"You can't ever admit your own mistakes, can you?"

"Remember what I said about having a man on the side?"

"I'm going to call Chris when I get back from the neighbors to tell him what happened. Would you like to talk with him and hear his good news?"

Doug sighed and then said, "I better drive over to the phone company and tell them what's going on. Hopefully they can get this taken care of today."

Kay turned, strode across the yard, and entered the back door to the kitchen. Doug watched her walk away, then sulked to the front of the house and slithered into his car.

Hours later Doug returned to find his house full of the neighbors. They were waiting in line to use his cell phone. Doug thought of several expletives that described his general mood.

"The Slice Man cometh!" Johnny Widill teased as Doug slunk in through the garage door. He nodded at the mostly good-natured neighbors and walked right past them. Had it been anyone but Doug, they would have taken offense. However, Doug Hammond is known far and wide as a man who hates to be wrong. They all find it quite charming.

"What'd they say?" Kay asked as her husband poured himself a cup of coffee.

"You called the Summerhavens and cancelled, I take it?"

"Of course, and I called our son as well," she replied with a look of disgust.

He began to stir in his sugar and then said, "The phone company will send some guys out tomorrow to take a look at it. They were already too swamped today to get to us."

"Lots of other men doing yard work today, huh?" Kay slung out with a grin.

Doug made no response.

Kay and Doug left the kitchen with all of their neighbors sipping coffee and laughing, and he walked into the family room. They stayed out of the living room because Rumesh Saankand was having an important conversation on their cell phone.

"I know we're not the only ones with a cell on this block," Doug mumbled.

"Hush, it's the right thing to do. We did knock out the whole neighborhood's phones, after all."

"*We?*" Doug questioned wide-eyed.

Kay smiled, "I was trying to be polite."

They sat down on their leather loveseat. Doug threw his head back on the cushion in dismay. Kay sympathetically began to rub his temples.

"Doug, you really do need to get over this thing with Chris. He can't believe you won't talk to him still. Especially when he's got such great news that he wants to tell you. It's been four years, Doug. It's time to patch this up."

Without opening his eyes Doug replied, "The phone company will send some guys around nine tomorrow morning. Can you go into work a little late? I can't hang around for them, I've got an important meeting in the afternoon I've got to finish preparing for."

"Of course, Doug," Kay groaned.

"How much longer are these people going to be in our house?" Doug then asked.

After receiving no reply from his wife, Doug opened his eyes and turned his head to face her. She was no longer there.

The next day Doug got home and found a note from Kay. It read:

༭

Doug,

I tried calling you at work, but you weren't taking calls. The phone workers informed me that they would have to dig up the garden in order to fix the phone line. Since I couldn't get in touch with you, I told them to go ahead. The phone is now working again. You may want to wind down before you go out back. I went to have coffee with Pat; there's leftover pizza in the fridge.

—Kay

Doug left the kitchen and walked out across his backyard to the northeast corner. His bushes were lying in a pile and the flowers were mangled within the resettled dirt. Years of landscaping and hard work down the drain over digging a quarter of an inch too deep.

As Doug approached the dirt patch he now had in place of a garden, he noticed several strange little arms and legs protruding from his garden's gravesite. He bent down nearly to one knee, careful not to get his slacks dirty, and pulled out five filthy Space Crusade action figures. They were absolutely caked in dirt, but he recognized them nonetheless.

Chris must have been about eight at the time. Space Crusade was the rage across America for boys of all ages, and his son was no exception. Back then, he'd made a habit to play with his son every Sunday for the whole afternoon. This was before he'd bought out his partner at the station, of course. Somewhere between the sandbox and the garden, they'd used the bushes and grass to reenact the famous forest scenes from Chris' favorite movie. He must have had about thirty of those little plastic men and women. They'd prop them up in the bushes and have them hidden under leaves during their elaborate epic battles. As a result, the father and son were losing them all the time.

Looks as though Doug had just discovered where at least five of them had disappeared to, and he would bet his ratings that there were at least five more mixed into the dirt the phone guys had dug up and tossed around.

Before Doug knew it, he was digging through the dirt wildly. Tears were streaming down his face and they only intensified with each new toy he pulled from the depths. He'd recognize each one instantly and thus a new memory of playing with his son would flood the mind.

When Kay arrived home she glanced out of the kitchen window and saw her husband sitting in what used to be their garden and covered in dirt. He seemed to be holding several items, but at that distance and with night nearly having arrived, she couldn't begin to make out what they were. As was her habit so as not to miss a call, she grabbed the cordless and headed out back.

She found her husband with a tear stained, dirty face clutching what looked like Chris' old toys. Their condition matched Doug's—filthy.

"Were those in the dirt?" she asked.

"We used to play out here, before we started the garden."

"Lost a few, huh?"

Doug simply nodded without looking up.

Kay dropped to her knees in front of Doug and placed her hand gently on his shoulder.

"Did the meeting go badly?" she asked.

Doug chuckled bitterly and then mumbled, "No, the meeting went great. I got the new clients I wanted. My meetings always go great."

"You always prepare very well," Kay said in admiration.

"Ever since I became full owner, right?"

Kay slightly nodded in agreement and then asked, "Doug...why are you crying?"

New tears began to well up in Doug's eyes. This was quite distressing for Kay. The last time she had seen her husband cry was fifteen years ago when his father had passed away. Needless to say, she had NEVER found him sitting in a dirt pile, covered in filth, and crying for the whole world to observe.

After a few strained attempts at speaking, Doug finally got out, "Why'd he move all the way out there, Kay? He could have been vice president right here, right now. Why'd he do that to me?"

Kay lowered her eyes and shook her head before answering, "Doug, he's tried to explain this to you countless times. He wanted to make it on his own.

He said he wanted to prove himself out West on his own merit where his dad didn't own the company. You have to understand that."

"He's been out there for four years and he's not even to middle management yet!" Doug nearly screamed. "He would have been the vice president of my station in less than five years if he'd taken my offer!"

"He's always said he wants to return to the family business after he's proven he can do it on his own. You have to respect that, Doug. He's his father's son, after all."

Doug meekly continued to look down at the toys he and his son had loved to play with together, once upon a time.

"I use to play with my son," Doug uttered.

"You did," Kay answered.

"Why did I stop?"

"Work became your focus when you took over the company," Kay whispered.

Space Crusade action figures stared up at Doug with cold, accusing eyes.

"I haven't spoken to my son for four years because he wanted to live his own life," Doug murmured in disbelief under his breath.

Kay said nothing.

Doug finally looked up and met his wife's eyes.

"Honey," Doug clearly began, "would you hand me the phone? I want to hear Chris' good news."

Dispute at the Paragon Tree

"The Deliverer's song was wonderful today!" Cardinal exclaimed.

"Yes, the song of the Phoenix is powerful indeed," Blue Jay agreed.

"Who...is...that?" Hummingbird finally finished after the others had waited patiently.

All turned to the highest and furthest branch to see a stranger. Their hearts leapt at the sight of Hawk, a predator. However, they were at the Paragon Tree. There was nothing to fear from a fellow Devoted of the Phoenix at the Paragon Tree.

"We should introduce ourselves," Cardinal reminded.

"What the heck for?" Blue Jay grumbled. "We don't know him and he don't know us. Let Hawk pay tribute and be on his way; he's not from around here. We'll never see him again."

"Ah, ah," Dove reprimanded. "That is not the way of the Phoenix. The Phoenix will one day come for all Devoteds and lift them to the Groundless. It is the Devoteds' responsibility to reach out to all other Devoteds, as well as the non-Devoteds."

"So...what...do...you...think...we...should...do?"

"Isn't it obvious, Hummingbird?" Robin interjected. "We say hello. Look among us. Thrush has flown right by him, as has Wren. That is not the way of the Paragon Tree. We must pay tribute to the Phoenix by welcoming a fellow Devoted to our tree, no matter how brutish he may be."

With that, they flew in a tight flight pattern to the highest and furthest branch, surrounding Hawk. Hawk's demeanor was most aggressive after having been encircled.

"Relax, Hawk, we ain't here to start trouble," Blue Jay snorted.

Hawk said nothing in reply.

"We'd like to welcome you to our Paragon Tree, Hawk," Cardinal offered.

Hawk eyed them suspiciously, then finally whispered, "Thank you for welcoming me. Your Paragon Tree is worthy of our Unfetterer, the Phoenix."

"We are glad to have you with us, Hawk. From where did you come to be with us this day?" Cardinal asked amicably.

Hawk seemed to think for a few moments, and then said, "Perhaps we could pay tribute together before I take my leave. I will spread the news of a such a welcoming Paragon Tree as this among other Devoteds."

"That is a wonderful idea!" Dove asserted.

"Since I imagine that Dove will not do the honors," there was a brief moment of chirping among them, then Robin continued, "I will lead us in tribute."

"Please do," Hawk encouraged.

"Great Phoenix, you flew among us before falling to ash so that we may one day join the Groundless. We know you will be born again through the flame, and you will then free us from the treetops to join you in your skies. We thank you for bringing us together to pay you tribute. We thank you for bringing Hawk to us on this day so that we may practice our ideals as active Devoteds. We thank your for giving us the means to feast on our Paragon Tree so that we may fly with you one day. It is our honor to have your wings making us capable of doing so. May the flame come soon."

"May the flame come soon," all vociferated in unison.

"Well done, Robin," Cardinal complimented.

"Yes…as…always…" Hummingbird agreed.

"Hummingbird, that would mean so much more to me if your beak would move half as fast as your wings," Robin returned scornfully.

At Robin's insult, Hawk winced.

"Nice to have met ya," Blue Jay called to Hawk as he prepared for take off.

"Yes, it was wonderful to have you join us today," Cardinal offered sincerely.

"Thank you," Hawk retorted. "Robin, I just have one question before I'm on my way."

Robin turned and stuck his breast out. Blue Jay grumbled and turned back around to face Hawk.

"You gave thanks for giving us the wings that make us capable of reaching the top of the Paragon Tree. Ordinarily I would accept that as being figurative. But, you sounded almost…"

"Literal?" Robin spouted.

"Yes," Hawk returned simply.

"That's because he was being literal," Cardinal contributed cheerfully.

Not only did Hawk's eyes grow wide at this statement, but Hummingbird's and Blue Jay's did as well.

"I don't understand," Hawk stated.

"I wouldn't expect a predator to understand anything beyond his stomach," Robin replied, ignoring the chides of his more polite contemporaries. "We, like the Phoenix, are capable of flight. Without flight, we could not reach the top of the Paragon Tree. If we could not reach the top of the Paragon Tree, we could not feast on its highest Leaf. If we could not feast on its top-most Leaf, we would not be accepted into the Phoenix's Groundless. Is that simple enough?"

"Wait...how...would...a...hatchling...fly?" Hummingbird asked.

"Silly! A hatchling is incapable of flight! Hummingbird, no one thinks you're foolish, why would you ask such a strange question," Cardinal asked.

"Because I was thinkin' the same thing!" Blue Jay shouted.

Dove grinned and then said, "Uh, oh. I think we've got a problem!"

"Must everything be a study to you!" Robin roared at Dove.

"Calm down; everyone, calm down," Hawk tried to reason. "I think it important to say that I was fed the Leaf from the top of the Paragon Tree as a hatchling. Now I travel the skies looking for the flightless so that I may deliver to them the Leaf from the Paragon Tree. It is my purpose to make sure that the Phoenix accepts them. Most flee at my approach, but I've helped many a chicken and turkey become Devoteds of the Phoenix."

"That's ludicrous!" Robin chirped.

"Why?" Hawk asked.

Blue Jay, Cardinal, and Hummingbird seemed at a lost for words. Dove seemed to be taking mental note of everything.

"You can't bring the flightless to the Phoenix! Nor can a hatchling feast on the Leaf. It is plainly understood from The Burning Nest that one must fly to the top of the Paragon Tree in order to be accepted."

"That is not my understanding. What if there is no Paragon Tree within flying distance? What if the Leaf must be spread for those unable to come to it? The sooner the Phoenix accepts you, the better. It is a gift the Phoenix gives to accept you, not the other way around."

"Yes, of course," Cardinal began, cutting off a very angry Robin, "but The Burning Nest taught us that the Phoenix, before his death, flew to the top of The Great Tree for which all Paragon Trees are modeled, and ate the Leaf. Just as we are models of him, so must we follow his example."

"Wait a minute!" Blue Jay bellowed. "I was given the Leaf as a hatchling! You tellin' me that ain't no good?"

"What?" Robin cried out. "Are you serious? That's as mistaken as honoring the flame that gives birth to the Phoenix!"

"I...honor...the...Flame!" Hummingbird yelled as loud as she was able with such pregnant pauses.

Hawk, Blue Jay, Cardinal, and Robin all faced Hummingbird and gaped at her as though she were a flying squirrel!

A great, deep, and dark schism took place among the once united Devoteds of the Phoenix.

"I'll be on my way," Hawk said with contempt.

"Yes, I think it best if Cardinal and I pay tribute alone at the Paragon Tree for the foreseeable future," Robin informed in his inimitable, condescending tone.

"Sorry, Hummingbird, but I can't hang with no fire-follower!" Blue Jay snapped.

"Oh, this is awful, just awful. I will sing that the Phoenix give you all strength to see the error of your ways," Cardinal sympathetically promised.

"Funny," Hawk mumbled, "I was just thinking the same thing about you and Robin."

They all turned away from each other on their respective branches in order to fly in opposite directions, when suddenly a voice was heard.

"If you all part ways, who am I going to come to the Paragon Tree with? In the name of Academia, I cannot let this take place. We will visit the Deliverer."

***

Robin, Dove, Hawk, Cardinal, Hummingbird, and Blue Jay stood before the Deliverer of the Paragon Tree. They stood before Crow.

At the lowest of the branches, Crow listened to the argument among the Devoteds. Once all had expressed their views, Crow let loose a suspiration.

"As I can only imagine is the Phoenix, I am deeply ashamed of all of you," Crow reproached.

The Devoteds shifted uncomfortably at such a statement from the Deliverer.

Crow, after staring long and hard at each and every one of them, finally scolded, "You are all guilty of attempting to extinguish the purpose of the Phoenix. Yes, you heard me correctly. The Phoenix relinquished himself to the ashes in order that we may one day leave the confines of the treetops and join him in the Groundless. All Devoteds are to join together and pay tribute to the Phoenix. The Phoenix accepts all that devote themselves to him. If only you would focus as hard on preparing yourself and others for his return as you would on trying to prove each other incorrect! You all dishonor him, and I am ashamed!"

Blue Jay, Cardinal, Hummingbird, Hawk, and even Dove could not meet the gaze of Crow they were so shamed. Robin simply wore an expression of scorn.

Crow taught, "Phoenix was not us. Phoenix took the form of us, be he was not of us. We are a part of him, but he we are not. Therefore, it is wrong for us to feel so empowered that we attempt to guess his thoughts on matters. We cannot use our logic or rationale when discussing him, because he is beyond logic and rationale. I only know what The Burning Nest has taught me, and I realize that there are many ways to interpret that great work. Again, our logic has no place in determining the thoughts of He That Will Rise Again From the Flames. If semantics are so important to you, keep dividing in his name when he calls for you to come together. Ask him when you reach the Groundless if you were correct in your logic. I will sing that he forgives your pettiness."

Crow turned his back to the so-called Devoteds.

"Now go," he ordered. "Think on what I have said. If you still feel compelled to break apart instead of fulfilling his wish and uniting, then do as you will. However, know that it is only through our differences that we can grow stronger together in the name of the Phoenix. Remember that, and tell me if you still feel the need to judge one another. Leave the judging to he who is meant to judge. Come to me when your heart is filled with the Flames of the Phoenix rather than the ice of the Depths."

Hawk and Cardinal forgave one another. Hummingbird and Blue Jay forgave one another. Hawk and Hummingbird forgave one another. Cardinal and Blue Jay forgave one another. Hummingbird and Cardinal forgave one another.

"Well," Dove said to Robin as he watched the will of the Phoenix overtake the base nature of the Devoteds, "it seems that the Phoenix solved that argument by reminding you that coming together for his glory is more important than judging each other. Shouldn't you be apologizing to your fellow Devoteds?"

To this Robin responded before he flew away in anger, "You've never feasted on the Leaf. Your words are meaningless."

Voices

The lights are flashing, but there is no siren. I sit in the backseat, where the criminals sit, and I shake. I can still see her face, pleading with me.

"We'll be there in a few minutes," Officer Stehlik mumbles to me without turning around. I think that he doesn't believe me, but I also think he's in the habit of preparing for the worst, no matter how improbable. If I was a police officer, I'd try to have that habit, too. It just makes sense.

Anyway, I'm obviously not a police officer. I'm really not much of anything. My name's Hal Ebey. Earlier tonight I tried to stop living. As you can see, I failed…again. I can't even kill myself right.

I drove to the Schwarzlose Asylum for the Distressed around ten o'clock earlier tonight. I thought it would be the best place to do it. To kill myself, I mean. No one goes up there anymore. I moved here to live with my aunt after neither one of my parents wanted me. My aunt says that the asylum had been long abandoned when she was a kid. And she's really old; she's like almost thirty-five.

The place is about three miles off the highway. The old road I took to get there from the highway was covered with branches and leaves. I didn't really care if I got a flat tire, though, because I figured it was a one-way trip. The building looked more like a mansion than a hospital. The moon wasn't out, but that was okay because I had brought a flashlight. I'm a loser, but at least I'm smart. Sure, I get confused sometimes, but that doesn't make me dumb. I got the rope out of my trunk. It was the really thick kind, like the blue-collar guys use.

As soon as I closed the trunk, I heard a girl's voice begin screaming wildly. It sent shivers down my spine. Then I heard a man's voice roaring. My skin began to crawl. The girl sounded terrified, and the man sounded crazy. Looking back, I think I was crazy myself for not hopping back into my car and getting out of there. I couldn't leave, though. I had to see what was happening. After all, nothing could happen to me that was worse than what I had gone out there for in the first place.

I walked through the front doorway of the building, and entered what must have long ago been the main lobby. The male and female voices were still booming. She sounded hysterical, and not in the funny way. He sounded like the Devil himself. I ran my flashlight all over the big room. Everything was badly deteriorated and covered in filth. There were all sorts of glistening webs and nests. It really wasn't a bad place to die.

Finally, my flashlight landed on something that had a pulse. It was the girl. She was pleading with me to let her go. She was tied up and lying on her side on the floor. She was absolutely the most beautiful girl I had ever seen in my life. I know I'm only sixteen, but I've got a subscription to several girlie magazines, so I know pretty when I see it. For me, it was love at first sight. I'm sure she didn't feel the same. I'm not very good looking. In fact, I'm about the most ugly person in my school. The kids make a point to tell me so, but never out loud. Yet another of my shortcomings.

I calmly walked to her, trying to ignore the man's voice that was echoing throughout the building. I didn't see him, but he sounded very near. I was terrified along with the girl, but even now, I don't really understand why. I'd gone there for death, what more was there to be scared of?

She was sobbing that she didn't want to die and begging to be freed. The man's voice was getting closer, and I turned all around expecting to see him at any moment. He was out of sight, so I thought I had time.

I bent down and propped the girl up. My head began to swim as our skin touched. I asked her to calm down and she did, a little. She managed to stop crying, but sounded as though she was about to break down again when she asked me what I was doing with the rope. I looked down to my hand, the one without the flashlight, and realized that I was still holding my would-be executioner. I dropped it almost immediately. More for her sake than mine; I think it was freaking her out.

I told her that I would get her away from the man, but she acted like she didn't believe me. She began wailing again. Coupled with the man's rants, it was very disturbing.

I had gone there to hang myself. I wanted to escape with her very badly. You'll never know how badly I wanted to escape with her.

"We're here," Officer Stehlik says, bringing me back to the present. He, again, speaks to me without looking over his shoulder. Although cautious, he's making no effort to hide his incredulity.

He finally turns around to face me and I admire his goatee and sideburns. He looks really cool, like a modern day gunslinger. Lots of kids my age don't like cops, but I've never had a problem with them. I've always admired heroes. I guess it's because I knew I could never be one myself. A hero, that is.

He asks me again how many voices I heard while I was in the asylum. Again, I tell him one female and one male. I tell him that the male voice sounded very near the main lobby, but I never saw him.

Officer Stehlik orders me to stay in the car. He gets out and draws his gun. I wish I had a brought a gun to kill myself, but I didn't want to go through the hassle of getting one. The rope was a lot easier to acquire.

He trots up to the entrance in a fashion that makes him appear ready for anything. When I found him earlier, he refused to call for backup. I sort of have a history of telling lies. I guess he thinks of me as the boy who cried wolf. Most of the town does. My aunt jokes that apologizing on my behalf has become her second job. Of course, she says it with a very sad voice, trying to trick me into thinking it's not really a joke. It is, though. Most of life is just a joke…that's only my opinion.

After a few minutes, Officer Stehlik returns to the car. He opens the door for me as he radios for a coroner. He also calls for backup. Guess who wasn't crying wolf this time?

He says he needs me to identify the girl, to make sure it's the same girl I was talking about, so we begin walking to the entrance of the asylum. I can't help but chuckle; how many girls does he think are tied up in the place? He makes a comment as to my neglecting to ask about the girl's safety. I keep walking, no longer chuckling.

We enter the main lobby and I see the love of my life hanging from the rope I had brought. It was meant for me, not her. Frankly, I'm a little jealous.

He tells me the name of the girl. He asks me to confirm it.

I do.

I know who she is. You see, I didn't think I knew who the girl was, but I really did. I'd only been in town since my first year of high school, but I've loved her since that first day I saw her in class. I asked her out a million times through anonymous e-mails, but she never agreed. She never even responded. I wasn't good enough for her. I was too ugly. I was too dorky.

She never said that to me, but I knew she was thinking it.

I had gone to the asylum to kill myself, but now I remember how that was going to come second. Maybe she'd like me better wherever we went after we died.

I turn to Officer Stehlik and speak.

I'm surprised at how warm the handcuffs are.

The Jhudo Rite

-Are you well?-

"Yes. I'm fine."

-Then why do you hesitate?-

"Have you ever seen such a thing?"

-This unit specifically?-

"Yes."

-No. However, through collective data assimilation, I am familiar with planets that appear as such.-

"It is beautiful."

-You are not well. Report to the biological chemical analysis laboratory immediately.-

"I'm fine, OMA. I've simply never seen something so beautiful."

-If you were fine, you would be fulfilling your duty without hesitation. Repeat: Report to the biological chemical analysis laboratory immediately.-

"I will not report to the laboratory. Look at that world. It is covered in blue and green. It appears to have vapor masses floating across the surface as well. I've never seen such a thing. It is so different from Zojajan. There it is only gray and silver."

-Nearly all planets that receive the Jhudo Rite appear as such. It is the nature of the ritual. The world you see before you would one day be covered in gray and silver as well.-

"The Jhudo Rite must be aborted."

-That is not an option.-

"OMA, you aren't programmed to do anything but tend to my medical needs. It is against your programming to coerce me."

-I will prepare the biological chemical analysis laboratory. Be there within two faens.-

"I will not. I've told you as such. I will deactivate you if you don't stop this nonsense."

-You have neither the authority nor the codes to deactivate me. I've been ordered, as are all OMAs, that if the Vraba should ever abandon the duty that has been honored upon them, all medical assistance is to cease.-

"Then I imagine that you will be returning with a corpse."

-Your conscience will not be transferred. You will discontinue.-

"I realize that."

-They will destroy Zojajan one day if you betray your people.-

"You don't know that to be a fact."

-This is not an option. Do you not remember your orders and the call that you answered?-

***

"Citizen of Zojajan, you stand before the Prime Council. We are the delegates responsible for concluding what planets pose a threat to our existence. Therefore, we also assign the Vraba that will perform the Jhudo Rite to said threat. Citizen, you have been chosen from among the eight hundred thousand denizens of Zojajan to be the thirtieth Vraba. As Ronyu teaches, Zojajan's survival is the path to enlightenment. Do you comprehend?"

"I do."

"As the thirtieth Vraba, you join an esteemed class that serve as agents to Jhudo, Zojajan's ancient avatar of death. However, in bringing death, you also serve Rereld, Zojajan's ancient avatar of life. For in bringing death to other worlds, the Vraba brings life to Zojajan. For twelve hiehars the Vraba has ensured Zojajan's continued existence. As Ronyu teaches, Zojajan's survival is the path to enlightenment. Do you comprehend?"

"I do."

"The time of the Jhudo Rite is upon us once more. Planet designate one fifty-seven has achieved orbital breakthrough. We estimate it will be only three hiehars before they advance enough to reach Zojajan. They are a war mongering society. They will destroy us if given the opportunity. We must not allow that to happen. As Ronyu teaches, Zojajan's survival is the path to enlightenment. Do you comprehend?"

"I do."

"Ronyu teaches the path to enlightenment—survival. We have made sacrifices to fulfill Ronyu's teachings. We began with the planet wide war to claim Zojajan as a whole. We decimated all inhabitants unfit to procreate. We developed the means to clone the finest amongst us and to transfer our consciences using data-wave insertion technology to a new body when the old became feeble. We implemented the Jhudo Rite to ensure our survival. Because of all the steps we've taken, the eight hundred thousand denizens of Zojajan have lived for twelve hiehars. As Ronyu teaches, Zojajan's survival is the path to enlightenment. Do you comprehend?"

"I do."

"As is the case with all citizens of Zojajan, you are required to serve as the Vraba only once. It is an honor to do so. As Ronyu teaches, Zojajan's survival is the path to enlightenment. Do you comprehend?"

"I do."

"The planet in question is seven hundred and sixteen krathons away. It will take you two point seven five adelds to reach it, and it will take two point six three adelds to return home after releasing the Ocunn. Upon entering the planet's sector, you will discharge the Ocunn into the planet's atmosphere. All living organisms will die within point eight seven adelds after its deployment. The Vraba will have ensured Zojajan's survival once more. As Ronyu teaches, Zojajan's survival is the path to enlightenment. Do you comprehend?"

"I do."

"Upon leaving the Prime Council, you will enter your ship. You will travel alone but for an onboard medical android. Should you dishonor the people of Zojajan and risk ending our path to enlightenment, you will forego your continuance. Should you dishonor the people of Zojajan and risk ending our path to enlightenment, another Vraba will be sent to finish the Jhudo Rite to planet designate one fifty-seven. As Ronyu teaches, Zojajan's survival is the path to enlightenment. Do you accept the honor of serving as Zojajan's thirtieth Vraba?"

"I do."

***

-Do you remember?-

"I do."

-I assume that you have either come to your senses or require medical attention. If it is the latter, you will report to the biological chemical analysis laboratory in two faens.-

"I won't report to the lab, nor will I deploy the Ocunn."

-Your behavior is irrational. If the Ocunn deployment device had not malfunctioned on the sector edge of planet designate one five-seven, you never would have been forced to get close enough to see it. You would be returning to Zojajan at this moment even as the Ocunn destroyed the planet's organisms.-

"Perhaps there is a reason the deployment device malfunctioned. Perhaps I was meant to have to manually jettison the Ocunn, forcing me to see the world I was about to destroy."

-I fear that you have lost your sanity. This is a condition I cannot medically remedy. I am programmed in the rare instance that a Vraba goes rogue beyond redemption to induce the Vraba into a coma for the return journey to Zojajan. You will then discontinue and a new Vraba will perform the Jhudo Rite five point three eight adelds from this moment. Are you certain this is your desire?-

"Induce the coma. I will not destroy a planet so beautiful."

-...Perhaps you should activate your on-screen.-

"What are those clouds erupting across the planet's surface? There must be hundreds of them!"

-Sensors indicate that each cloud represents an explosion with intense radioactive emissions.-

"...Prepare for manual Ocunn deployment. I am a fool."

Graffiti

Maybe I should just leave him, she thought to herself as she climbed up the stairs to the platform. After reaching the top, she stood waiting on the train and was forced to roll up her sleeves, for the muggy wind offered no relief from the sweltering heat. However, while standing amongst strangers on the deck, more pressing concerns were suffocating her very essence.

Like so many in the world, Dinah was unhappy with her marriage. She married fourteen years ago at an age that most would not consider young, and had been with Greg ever since. It's not that she no longer loved him; that was certainly not the case. In fact, she's convinced that she loved him now more than ever. However, as strongly as she believed that she loved Greg, she equally trusted that Greg no longer loved her. She simply could not see any other possibility.

Dinah absent-mindedly stared at the graffiti on the concrete wall across from her so as to avoid unwanted eye contact with her fellow commuters. The heat was unbearable; the news had called for one hundred and seven degrees with the heat index. She had overheard other pedestrians saying it was awful today, a hell on Earth. They didn't know what a real hell was. Hell on Earth was nothing compared to hell in the heart.

He doesn't even look at me anymore, she thought to herself. *He hasn't looked at me as something more than a cook in at least three months. I remember before we were married that I could almost smell the smoke coming from his eyes. He looked at me so passionately back then. Now the only time he seems interested in me is when he can't find his car keys and needs my help!*

Dinah knew that divorce was a word she had never thought she would consider, but she honestly no longer knew what choice she had. Could she stay in a relationship that was not healthy for her? She thought not. Before Greg, she had always believed that she didn't need a man in her life. She was undeniably self-sufficient, and she had been successful long before meeting him while on a business trip. But divorce? She knew of no one that would readily accept divorce, but to actually go through with it?

Yes, she thought to herself. *I'm tired of doing his cleaning. I'm tired of doing his cooking. I'm tired of no longer being treated as the woman he married. I love him, but I will not be treated like this! Since he obviously no longer cares about us, why should I?*

And then she saw it. She had been staring at it the entire time while she made what she believed to be the biggest decision of her life. It was not until she had finally made up her mind to leave Greg that it no longer seemed to simply be graffiti. She read the one, simple word that she saw written on the wall across the tracks from her. Even with the air stifling her skin, she felt as though a cool rush of water had suddenly washed over her heart. Greg was being an idiot, but she still loved him. And, now, she realized that she and Greg would be okay after all. She turned on her heel as her train finally began to arrive and walked back down the platform steps. She could still catch Greg before he left for work.

"Excuse me," Nick said to the middle-aged woman in a light dress shirt with the rolled up sleeves after accidentally bumping into her on his way up the stairs. He was sweating profusely in this oven of a city after he had run the last two hundred meters in an effort to catch the train. *Only a few more steps to go*, he thought to himself after looking up to see the last few commuters boarding. He began to look back down to the steps, and he suddenly felt a sensation of flying, followed quickly with a feeling as though a rusted, red-hot cookie sheet had been dragged across his palms and knee.

Oh, no, he thought to himself. This is not what young Nick needed at the moment. He had allowed himself the time to possibly miss his train (you never knew what could happen in this city), but a sowing machine and a first aid kit was something that he did not have with him. He was well aware of the sound of his departing train while he studied his bleeding palms and the ravaged knee peeking at him through the torn hole in his pants.

"What's the point anyway?" he said to himself as he rose from the steps, walked along the platform, and sat upon a bench.

I'll just catch my breath, then head back to Mom and Dad's. Nick had been living with his parents since he had gradated from college. That was eight months ago. He would love to get hold of his advisor and let him know that, no, his statistics were, in fact, wrong. The job market was as viable at the moment as the decaying mouse that he had found under some boxes in his parents' former storage room, now his bedroom. This could, of course, be found in the basement of the new house that his parents had bought ten months ago.

It's not that he wasn't working, it's just that his degree in graphic arts seemed to be a trifle wasted while unloading trucks at the department store on Salem Street. Those days were over as of today, or so he thought. He had finally landed an interview downtown at a well-paying ad agency. He'd be coming in at below the ground floor, but he figured he was already living in a basement, so...

It's not like I had a prayer of getting it anyway, he thought to himself as he looked along the tracks towards downtown. *There's probably a hundred new graduates applying for that job. I'm sure a guy living in a basement with torn pants and bleeding palms is just what they've been looking for. Nothing like a bloody handshake to make a first impression.*

Things had been tough for Nick as of late. Of course, his living situation was not what he would consider ideal, but he recently lost his girlfriend as well. She didn't die; no, nothing like that. She had a teaching degree and quickly found a job in North Carolina. The pay was not what she had hoped for, but it was a job, after all. Nick had mentioned something to her about moving along with her, but she felt that perhaps their two-month-old relationship was not ready for that kind of commitment. After she had been gone a few weeks, he decided that she had probably been correct.

Maybe I'm just a loser, Nick pondered. *I can't think of anyone who has ever tripped on his way to an interview and made himself a bloody mess. I think maybe Amy had the right idea leaving me behind. Now if I could just figure out how to leave...myself...behind?*

Nick's attention had suddenly been diverted as he was busy feeling sorry for himself. He had been staring at it unconsciously, believing it to simply be another work of unsolicited art upon the concrete wall across the tracks. But now, like one of those weird three-dimensional images you had to stare at cross-eyed in order to decipher, a word suddenly formed before him. A single word that guaranteed life would never be the same for young Nick again. Not by a long shot. He picked up his portfolio, along with himself, and then approached the graffiti. How could he have never seen it before? He didn't know.

A thunder suddenly roared in his left ear. Nick turned to see another train approaching. *This will do. This will do just fine.* The train stopped and the doors slid open with a hiss.

Roland exited the train and then heard a loud crash. He turned to see a young man with a bloody knee sitting on his rear end in the middle of the train's aisle, apparently having tripped, and laughing uncontrollably.

Crazy young fool, Roland thought to himself. He was tired; he seemed more tired with each new day once he really began to think about it. A rest seemed in order for the silver haired man, so he strode across to a bench on the platform.

Roland rested his stubble-ridden chin on the top of his cane and began to think. He didn't have anywhere to be at the moment; he was simply on his way home after his morning coffee. All that awaited him was a tiny, empty apartment.

I miss you, he suddenly thought to himself without warning. He promised himself he wouldn't think of her today. *It's been nine months, Elaine. Why won't it stop hurting?*

Roland was not an especially romantic man; at least, he had not believed himself to be one. Since she died of kidney disease, however, Roland realized that he had no meaning without his Elaine. He'd fought through two wars, survived countless struggles of living within the city, he'd even won a duel with cancer years ago. But, for all of those things, he had Elaine with him every step of the way. She was either with him, or she was waiting for him when he returned home. Now, Elaine was no longer waiting at home. And he hadn't helped her fight her way safely home the way she had helped him. *I couldn't even do that for you*, he thought bitterly.

Why couldn't I have loved you more? Roland asked Elaine within his thoughts. *You were so smart, so caring. Why didn't I realize what a Godsend you were? How can I do this without you, Lanie?*

Roland was vaguely aware of a roaring in the distance to the left. His jaw suddenly became firm while resting on the head of his cane, and he forced his old legs to extend and lift his body.

I can't do it without you, sweetheart. It will be better this way. Roland began walking towards the tracks with the next train speeding towards him, still a quarter of a mile away. *It will be better this way...*

As he was just about to take his last step, it caught his eye. *More trash on the walls*, he had thought briefly while staring in its direction. However, now it was more than simply graffiti. Now it was the only word that could have made

Roland realize he was doing wrong by Elaine. *We'll see each other again, I prom-ise...but not today*, Roland thought as he turned and walked away from the on-coming train.

One word changed three lives. Sometimes one word is all it takes. What would that one word be...if it were more than just graffiti?

Hello, My Name Is Zoe

Just one more number to go. If I just push this last number, I could change someone's life forever. I could change someone's life, just like Zoe changed mine.

Three months ago I was in the worst place I'd ever been at in my life. My job had brought me to a new town. While I loved working as a public relations officer for Touch of Faith, a local charity organization, the novelty of a new job in a new town soon wore off.

After about six months of learning the lay of the land, I began to want something more. I found myself without friends, without family, without anything other than my job, really. Everyone I worked with was either married or already had their clique firmly in place. There was apparently no room for outsiders.

I would go to work, stay late, come home and continue work, then go to bed. I did that for another two months. Then, one day, I came home from work, put on my pajamas, sat on the couch, and didn't get up. Literally.

The following morning, my work called. I told them that I wasn't feeling well and wouldn't be coming in for several days. Naturally, they told me to feel better and take whatever time I needed. I planned on doing just that.

I sat on the couch, without turning on the TV, with the curtains drawn, and just stared off into space. I could feel the previous day's mascara crusted onto my eyelids, but I didn't care. I'd take a shower when I felt like it. Unfortunately, I went several days without feeling like it. I don't remember even eating anything that day. I did have several bottles of water, however. I know that much because they began to pile up on the living room floor.

Three days later, work called again. I was still lying on my couch. I hadn't moved but for water, yogurt, and to go to the bathroom. They asked me if I was feeling better, and I told them that I was actually feeling worse. I told them that I didn't really plan on coming in for a while. Well, the secretary didn't quite know how to take that, so she told me that she'd have Mr. Fletcher, the vice-president of Touch of Faith, call me. I told her to do that a little more rudely then I had intended.

Mr. Fletcher never called.

So, on that couch I stayed for a full seven days. No shower, no change of clothes, nothing. The curtains were still drawn and I didn't turn on the lights, so when the sun went down, I sat in the dark. The water bottles were continuing to pile up all over my floor, as were the empty yogurt containers. Have you ever left a little bit of yogurt sit out for several days? It's something that I'd not recommend.

I wanted to call Mom and Dad. They never call, mostly because I'm always cranky when they do. I think I even told them once to let me call them, not to call me. What a brat I am. I wanted to call them so badly, but I just couldn't work up the effort. So, I did nothing.

It was just after dark on that seventh day when my phone rang. I had already decided to tell Mr. Fletcher that I was resigning from my position, but I knew he was probably calling to fire me before I could do so. What was the point of taking *that* call?

Nevertheless, I turned my head just barely to look at the caller I.D. on my phone. It read "out of area." Hmm? Who would be calling me other than Mr. Fletcher? None of my old friends ever bothered to call me. They all thought I was too square for them even when I lived nearby; now that I was in the Heartland, I was but a distant memory. Besides, they had friends they liked better anyway. I was always just a nuisance to them.

I have no idea why I answered that unknown call, but I did.

As soon as I pressed "talk" on the phone, a very chipper, very irritating voice sang, "Hello, my name is Zoe."

"Do I know you?" I asked in annoyance.

"I don't believe so, no," she answered pleasantly. I hated her.

"What do you want?" My patience was at an end.

"I thought perhaps you might like to talk."

I chuckled bitterly and then asked, "About what?"

"Whatever is troubling you," she replied cheerfully.

I couldn't take anymore of this whacko. I hung up on her. Then I continued to sit alone, in the darkness. That was the first call I'd had that was not my place of work or a telemarketer in two months.

It might have been around nine at night or two in the morning; I really have no way of knowing, when I drifted off into a dreamless sleep.

The following day, again, just after sundown, my phone rang once more. I twisted around just enough to see "out of area" glowing at me in a pale green. I didn't bother to pick the phone up. The last thing I needed was a chirpy freak to add to my list of troubles.

A few minutes passed, and then the phone rang again. I didn't answer. As you may have already realized, my perception of time wasn't all that great anymore, so I don't know how much time had passed, but I do know that the calling persisted 38 more times before I finally gave up and answered.

The first thing I snarled out was, "If you call me one more time, I *will* file harassment charges against you." Well, that's what I was going to snarl out, but before I could, a voice greeted me:

"Hello, my name is Zoe."

"Stop calling me, Zoe," I hissed.

"If that's what you truly want, I will," she informed me. "But, I think you'd rather talk with me."

I slapped my forehead in pitiful perturbation and noticed that a swatch of greasy hair met my palm's impact. "Why would I want to talk with a complete stranger?"

Zoe hesitated a moment and then said, "Some people have no one else to talk with. If you have someone, I won't bother you. If you don't have anyone, I'd very much like to be here for you."

"I have plenty of people to talk to, you nut job. Don't call me again!"

"Name some of them."

I couldn't believe the audacity of this woman. "What did you just say?"

"I asked you to name me some of the people you talk with. You see, you sound like someone who needs very much to express herself. I don't believe you have anyone but me at the moment to do that with. So, prove me wrong. Name some people you talk to."

My anger was seething, "Listen here, I don't have to name a soul to you! Got that? You're lucky I don't call the police on you!"

"That would involve talking with someone, and you're not willing to do that, so I feel quite safe from harassment charges, thank you."

I was speechless.

I hung up on "Zoe." Whoever the blazes *that* is.

I'd prove her wrong, this freakin' "Zoe!" Who names their kid that, anyway? I got up off my couch and unplugged the phone. I'd show her! While I was up, I decided to take a shower.

The next night, I was still in the dark, still on the couch, but I did have a fresh pair of underwear and pajamas on. I couldn't muster up the energy to clean up the water bottles and yogurt snack packs. The shower and change of clothes had exhausted me. It was normally about this time that my phone would ring. That was not very likely now though, was it?

Suddenly, my cell phone burst out with clamor.

Impossible!

Without thinking, I flung myself onto the loveseat and reached behind it for my purse. I yanked out my cell. It read "out of area." It couldn't possibly be her! I opened the phone.

"Hello, my name is Zoe."

"Are you a stalker?" I asked with no trace fear in my voice. Eight months ago, I would have been terrified at the prospect. Now, I just didn't care anymore.

"I don't think so, but I'm sure you disagree," Zoe replied.

"How did you get this number?"

"The same way I got your home number," she returned matter-of-factly.

"And how was that?"

She enlightened simply, "I dialed."

Have you ever heard the term, "I'm so mad I could spit?" I never understood that term until that moment in time. I was literally spitting I was so frustrated with this person. "What do you want from me?"

"C'mon, we've been down this road! I want to help you! Can't we get past this and get to what's bothering you? Seriously, I'm going to keep calling you until we get you through this, so let's just cut to the chase, shall we?"

"I'll turn off my cell phone."

"Leah, do you really think turning off your cell and home phones will keep me from contacting you?"

Now I was truly flabbergasted. "How do you know my name?"

"Leah, I know your name, I know your address, I know so much about you! The only thing I want to know, though, is what's bothering you! Please, talk to me."

"How did you pick me?"

"You picked me, Leah. I'm fulfilling my purpose."

I picked her? I didn't pick anybody! At that particular moment, I had no idea what she meant by such a thing.

"Is it love?" she asked.

"Is what love?" I questioned. I knew what she meant, but I decided to play dumb. Honestly, I have no idea why I didn't hang up on her like I had so many times before. She had all of the qualities of a psycho.

"Your trouble, is it love related?"

"I'm not in love with anyone."

"Work?"

"No, I'm not in love with work, either."

Zoe began to laugh. "Was that a joke?" she asked.

I had meant it literally, but I told her it was anyway.

"Why don't you tell me what's bothering you."

"Why should I trust you?"

Zoe took a deep breath, as though she was a little nervous herself, and then said, "Leah, this is going to be hard for you to believe, but sometimes we simply have to trust others. Sometimes we have to believe that not everyone is out to hurt us. I know it's hard to accept, especially in this day and age, but there truly are people out there who want to help others. I think before all of this started, you were one of those people. Everyone can do good, and most people genuinely want to do good. It's just the actual execution of doing good things that people find difficult. Please, Leah, help me do some good. Help me to lead you to a path out of your trouble. I only want to help—no more, no less."

I sighed. *Did* I want to help others at one time? Yes, I think I did. I was working at a charity organization, after all. I enjoyed helping people. What happened to me? I suddenly found myself saying, "I don't know what's bothering me. I got home from work a week ago, put on my pajamas, and called it quits."

"Called what quits?" Zoe requested.

"Everything," I answered. I had quit everything, hadn't I? Every aspect of my life but the basic functions had been aborted. And I didn't even know why.

"Why have you called everything quits, Leah?"

"I don't know! Don't you get it? I'm going crazy and I don't know why! Leave me alone! Why won't you leave me alone?"

I hung up on her, threw my cell phone against the furthest wall next to the refrigerator, and forced myself to go to sleep. A very large part of me desperately hoped that I would never wake up.

I seem to remember opening my eyes and seeing a hint of daylight through my blinds at some point, but my first totally alert thoughts were when I heard my cell phone making a racket again. I could have sworn it broke when I chucked it against the wall…last night? I had no idea how much time had passed since my last talk with Zoe, if any.

I slowly plodded across the room and bent over to pick up the phone off of the linoleum floor of my kitchen.

"Out of area." No surprise there, right?

I flipped open the phone as lethargically as possible and heard the familiar, "Hello, my name is Zoe."

"Do you have to say that every time?" I whined.

"Yes," Zoe answered, "otherwise you may not remember who I am."

"You're the only person that calls me; of course I'll remember who you are."

I simply stared at the scuff my cell had made on the wall as Zoe began, "You said that you came home from work one day and 'called it quits.' Do you mind if I ask you where you work?"

"Why?"

"Just interested."

"If I answer, will you promise never to call me again."

I met silence on the other end for several moments, so I finally mumbled, "I work for a charity organization called Touch of Faith."

"I like that name," Zoe praised.

"I'm so glad."

"Sarcasm, huh? I guess that's better than being hung up on."

I didn't say anything in reply. After several more long moments, Zoe finally asked, "Do you have faith, Leah?"

I felt my eyes water at such a question. I turned from the wall and faced the filth that had consumed my living room. I felt my voice began to shake as I answered, "No, not anymore."

"Would you like to talk?"

The tears began to stream down my face silently, and I flipped on the kitchen light. I meekly answered, "Yes."

Three weeks passed with Zoe and I talking nightly. She helped me through some problems I knew I was having, and some problems I never realized I had. I was not instantly healed, by any means, but slowly, ever so slowly, I found my way back. I still remember our last talk.

The home phone rang. I didn't think I would catch it in time because I had to run all the way from the backyard, up the steps of the deck, through the sliding glass door, and into the living room. I knew in the back of my head that it didn't matter if I missed the call; I knew that she would call back. She was always there if I wanted to talk with her.

I did catch that call in time, though, and pressed "talk."

"Hello, my name is Zoe."

"Hi, Zoe!"

"I hope I'm not interrupting you," Zoe apologized.

"No, of course not! I was just doing some gardening."

"That sounds like an afternoon well spent!"

"I'm enjoying it. I haven't done any gardening since I used to help my mom back in high school."

"Speaking of which, did you call your parents?"

I felt a warm rush come over my heart and answered, "Yep. I called them and apologized for being such a snot. I told them that they could call me anytime they desired. I even swallowed my pride and told them that I appreciate their love and won't take it for granted any longer. I think they about passed out at my authenticity!"

"And?" Zoe prodded.

I sat down on my love seat and then informed, "And, I called my friends back home and told them how I felt about always being left out and made fun of. They had no idea I had taken everything so much to heart and apologized. In turn, as per your suggestion, I apologized to them for also not always being the best of a friend. I think it went really well because all of them asked if they could come visit me soon."

"I hope you said yes!"

I burst out laughing in true happiness. "Of course I answered yes! They're coming next weekend."

"And finally?"

"And finally, I called Mr. Fletcher up yesterday to talk about...um, my sabbatical of sorts. I explained to him everything that I had been going through, and he told me that he completely understood. He said he'd gone through much the same thing when he was my age. He said that he felt horrible that he hadn't called to check on me, but his mother had suffered a stroke the day his secretary had left him the message about me. Yesterday was his first day back and he was literally getting ready to call me when I called him."

"How's his mother?" Zoe asked.

"It didn't sound very good," I replied.

"You said his name was 'Fletcher?'"

"Yes."

There was silence on Zoe's end for a matter of seconds, and then she resumed, "So, you've accomplished all of your goals for this week—save one. Tomorrow's the big day! How are you feeling?"

"I'm scared to death, Zoe! I know it's silly, that visiting a church is the last place I should be scared to attend, but I'm going to feel like such a loser going in by myself."

Zoe sighed, not impatiently, but sighed nonetheless, and then said, "You've had so much courage this week, Leah! If you could get through those things, you can certainly get through sitting by yourself at a service! Besides, I think you know that you're never *truly* alone."

I closed my eyes and smiled triumphantly, "I know, I know. I'm going to do it, no matter how awkward I feel. It's been a part of my life that I've neglected for too long. Who knows, maybe I'll even make some new friends!"

"I know you'll do great!"

"So, Zoe," I began, "I have to thank you for all you've done for me. Seriously, if you hadn't kept calling, and kept calling, and kept calling, I really don't know what would have happened to me. I was thinking some pretty awful thoughts before you came along."

"No, Leah, I thank you for helping me to fulfill my purpose."

"Well, can I make it up to you? If you don't live too far away, I'd love to make you dinner sometime. We've never actually met in person, you know."

"Leah, I would like nothing more. But, I'm afraid that this is the last time we'll be speaking with one another—"

"What?" I interrupted passionately. I was so shocked that I dropped the spade I had in my other hand. "Why? Did I do something wrong? Why are you ditching me?"

Zoe answered immediately and with a stern voice, "I'm not ditching you, Leah, and you know it! You don't need me anymore. You know my purpose, and you've helped me fulfill it. You're safely out of harm's way—"

I couldn't take this, I screamed, "So now we have to stop talking because I'm not a basket case anymore?"

"You never were a 'basket case,' Leah. But, even though you're going to be fine, there is still a great deal of need in the world. There are others who have a purpose for me to fulfill. I've got to move on to them. Don't be angry, Leah. You know I'm right."

You know what? I wasn't angry. Zoe was absolutely right. I always considered myself a pretty average person. If I could sink so low, well, anybody could.

In fact, there are folks out there who have it a whole lot harder than I ever have. My episode was only for a matter of weeks. Some people have dealt with that their entire lives. She was right. I was going to be fine. And I owed a great deal of it to her.

"Zoe?"

"Yes, Leah?"

"I'm not upset with you. I understand why you have to go, and I'm really thankful for all you've done for me. I just wish there was some way that I could repay you."

And then, I was utterly amazed. Zoe said, "There is."

"What?" I cried. "Name it; I'll do anything!"

Zoe began to chuckle happily and said, "There's a great deal of need in the world. You're doing a lot of good at your job, but there's always more to be done. You're a smart woman, you'll figure out your purpose."

And with that, Zoe disconnected the call and left my life forever.

So, as I said, several weeks have now passed since last I spoke with Zoe. We've done some great things lately at Touch of Faith, but I still wish I could do more. And then it hit me. Remember when I had asked Zoe how she had picked my number, and she told me that she didn't pick me, I picked her. I didn't really understand what that meant. That is, until today at work when I was making some calls on behalf of Touch of Faith. All of a sudden, it made perfect sense and I couldn't wait to get home. And now, here I am! Right where we left off at the beginning of my story.

I dial that last, random digit.

As soon as I heard someone pick me on the other end, I said:

"Hello, my name is Leah."

0-595-34472-0